A Collection of Paranormal Tales

MIDNIGHT RISING

A Zimbell House Anthology

Midnight Rising

A Collection of Paranormal Tales

A Zimbell House Anthology

For permission requests, write to the publisher:
"Attention: Permissions Coordinator"
Zimbell House Publishing
PO Box 1172
Union Lake, Michigan 48387
mail to: info@zimbellhousepublishing.com

© 2018 Zimbell House Publishing

Published in the United States by Zimbell House Publishing
http://www.ZimbellHousePublishing.com
All Rights Reserved

Trade Paper ISBN: 978-1-947210-60-8
Kindle ISBN: 978-1-947210-61-5
Digital ISBN: 978-1-947210-62-2
Library of Congress Control Number: 2018908916

First Edition: August 2018
10 9 8 7 6 5 4 3 2 1

ZIMBELL HOUSE PUBLISHING
UNION LAKE

Acknowledgments

Zimbell House Publishing would like to thank all those that contributed to this anthology. We chose to showcase seven new voices that best represented our vision for this work.

We would also like to thank our Zimbell House team for all their hard work and dedication to these projects.

Contents

Before the Dawn

Michael Grantham

One

It was five past sunset when she came to my office, all legs and a shy smile.

"Excuse me, Detective Cain," she said as she knocked on my door.

I shoved the novel I was reading into a desk drawer and invited her in. She moved to the middle of my office, her floral dress adding splashes of color I never knew I was missing. She looked around as if she were judging my ability by the wallpaper and her gaze stopped at an old photo of me and my dad in matching Las Vegas Police Department uniforms backlit by one of those sunsets you only get in the southwest.

"I was just about to lock up, but I'm not in any hurry," I said, "and please call me Ray."

I walked out from behind my desk and pulled out one of the chairs, motioning for her to make herself comfortable. When she did I sat on the edge of my desk, prepared to be the charming private detective, then she turned her baby blues on mine. She had dark hair, pale skin, and the figure of a runway model but those eyes gave me butterflies like Gina Rosenstein did in grade school.

I looked down and began rubbing at a non-existent spot on my desk.

"So how can I help you Miss …?"

"Rice, Laura Rice."

"What can I do for you, Laura?" My eyes drifted from the desktop to her legs, and it took considerable effort to return my focus to my desk.

"I was hoping you could help me find my sister."

"Have you gone to the police?"

"I have but," she said and paused for a practiced moment before continuing in a rush, "My sister is an adult and has skipped town before, so they said that there is little they can do."

It was the scripted way she said it that brought me back.

"Do you think your sister is in danger?" I asked as I walked back around to my side of the desk.

"I don't know," she said. "She always tells me when she needs to get away but not this time. I haven't heard from her for over a month."

That time I was sure I heard it. There was a lie in there. I steadied myself and looked her in the eye. She was still breathtaking, with an earnest look of worry on her perfect face. I held her gaze, focused on the lie, held it tight in my mind, and when I didn't flinch, I smiled.

"Is your sister a vampire too?"

Her earnest look fell just a little then she froze. It was an unnatural stillness like someone hit the pause button. It would have terrified me if I hadn't seen it a thousand times since the big vampire coming out.

"What gave me away?"

"Not much," I said. "You asked permission to come in, avoided looking in the mirror next to the door, and you moved to the center of the room away from the shelf where I'm using a rosary as a bookmark. When you looked around the room, the only thing that held your attention for longer than a second was the photo of the sunset. On top of that, you could be the most beautiful woman I've ever seen."

When I saw no reaction, I added, "You're looking for a detective, right?"

She was silent long enough for me to question my career choices.

"Yes, my sister is also a vampire," she said and brushed a strand of hair behind her ear for my sake. "Will that keep you from taking my case?"

"I'll tell you, I've noticed that your kind likes to keep to themselves."

Her eyebrows rose at the "your kind" comment and the corner of her mouth turned up just a bit. Again, I'm sure the movements were for my benefit, and I was glad she made an effort to appear human. It helped calm my nerves.

"You're right, detective. We like to handle our own business." She considered something, then her innocent girl act vanished. She held up an e-cigarette and asked, "May I?"

"Of, course."

The thin stream of vapor she blew out slid between invisible air currents and coiled behind her before vanishing.

"I asked for help from my kind. I spoke to those that work for the police, and I made an appeal to the local clan. Everyone told me to wait, to give it time. They spoke to me like I was newly made, like I did not know the moods and temperaments of my kind."

I could no longer tell if she was lying, but I could tell that Laura was in real pain and desperate for help. She wasn't putting on the shy, sexy act anymore and I'm embarrassed to admit that I found her despair almost as alluring.

"We were turned together. That's how we are sisters," she continued. Her eyes did not watch me, they looked out my window, the bright lights of the city reflecting in her eyes. "For hundreds of years, we have been near constant companions. When the big announcement was made, Barbara was ecstatic. She joined the masses and went to all the marches. She registered, and campaigned, and voted. Her happiness was profound, and it shone from every fiber of her being."

"Not you though," I said encouraging her to continue.

"No," Laura said. She gave a quick laugh before continuing. "I did not handle it well. My reclusive behavior became unhealthy. My paranoia grew to schizophrenic heights. I quit drinking the animal and synthetic, and I started living off what I could buy on the black market, which wasn't much and cost us a fortune."

"You're better now?"

"Barbara gave me an ultimatum. I could join her in this grand new world, or she would leave."

"So, she left?"

"No," she said. "I took the plunge. She held my hand as I registered. I got involved and helped the cause by designing posters and t-shirts. Have you seen the '*We don't want your life, we want the same rights,*' or '*Don't hate me because I'm 90?*' Those are my designs."

The look of happiness that came across her face made me question her sincerity. Was it just a show for my benefit? Either way, she was coming to the heart of the matter, so I remained quiet.

"We made friends. We began living a quasi-suburbanite dream. We felt alive." She exhaled a thick cloud that obscured her face; when it passed, it took with it every expression. "Then one night she went to drop off some campaign posters and never returned."

Her words hung in the air, thicker than the chemical clouds and more unyielding.

I pulled out my phone, closed several final notice messages, and began typing with a practiced speed.

"Do you have a photo of Barbara?" I asked, then remembered, vampires don't appear in photographs. I remember thinking it had to do with mirrors, but even digital photos come out as unrecognizable blurs. "Sorry."

She reached into her purse and pulled out a photo-realistic drawing of the two girls together. Barbara was as beautiful as Laura. It was easy to see how they could pass as sisters. They both had dark hair and pale skin, blue eyes and full lips but where Laura was sharp edges and serious features, Barbara was cherubic.

"You're taking the case?"

"What can I say? I'm a sucker for a damsel in distress." I realized the pun as soon as it was out. Laura gave me a wry smile, and I apologized again.

"It's okay. I understand the ... I understand," Laura said, leaving me to speculate what it was that she understood. That I was terrified of her, that I needed the job to be able to eat next week, or was it the fact that despite how hard I was trying to play it cool, I was excited to take this case.

I cleared my throat. "Where was Barbara going that night?"

"To the campaign office of James Chandler."

"Then that's where I'll start, but I have a couple more questions."

Two

It was still early evening when I walked Laura out of my building to a car that cost more than everything I own. The near-silent hum of the electric engine mixed with the rest of the traffic. Another smile, a wave, and the car drove away. I watched it turn the corner before I pulled out my phone and saw I had inefficient funds to order a car of my own. I kicked myself for not pushing for a higher retainer.

My mind was focused on the case as I walked to the bus stop. Laura wanted me to see Barbara as a girl who embraced the chance of returning to society with passion. She made a point of telling me that when she was at her low point, she bought blood, never admitting that she fed off humans. I found that hard to believe.

I made it a block and a half from my office when something struck me on the back of my head. I went down, got hit again, and went out. I came to between a couple dumpsters. A large man in a balaclava and hoody was leaning on my chest and slapping my face. A couple of his buddies were shuffling their feet behind him and twitching at every car that passed either end of the alley.

"Wake up sfigato," the man said, his breath was thick with garlic.

He stopped slapping me and looked deep into one eye then the other.

"There you are. Can you hear me?"

I tried to say that I did, but the pressure on my chest made it hard to speak. I nodded.

"Good, now hear this—Stay away from that fanger bitch. Whatever business you had with her is finished. Capiche?" The man made a fist in front of my face, a ram's head protruding from a large pinky ring less than an inch from my eye.

I nodded again, and the three men walked out of the alley leaving me slumped against the dumpster.

Getting to my feet took longer than it should have, and even then I was wobbly. I'd been knocked out before. I'd spent the majority of my youth fighting both in and out of the ring. I was never Golden Gloves, but I made more guys kiss the canvas than I ever did. The knot on the back of my head told me I was hit with some kind of a sap or a club.

As I staggered the rest of the way to the bus stop, no one offered me help. In fact, the few pedestrians I passed along the way gave me a wide berth, just another drunk staggering between casinos. At least I hope for society's sake that's why I was shunned.

In a small bit of luck, my bus arrived just as I did. I flopped into the first available seat and explored the lump on the back of my head as I considered the implications of what just happened. I figured either the Italians or one of the Hardline Humanists groups we call HH wanted me to stop looking for Barbara, but I didn't know why.

The rumor is that long before the coming out, the Italians were fighting the Vampires for control of Las Vegas. In the 1990's, some of the families 'in-the-know' of our supernatural friends decided to add some clever touches to entice wealthy vamps into the desert. They built large windowless buildings with vaulted ceilings painted to look like blue skies and lit the whole place to look like noon on a Sunday afternoon in spring. Vampires loved it so much they tried to buy the whole town.

The guy who jumped me was Italian, but the Families are subtler with their threats. Showing up at your favorite diner or offering you a ride across town then letting you know that you are not wanted without saying a word about it, that's more their style. It's classic, elegant, and far more intimidating than a thwap to the back of the head.

The thug's gracelessness wasn't the only tipoff either. HH'ers love garlic—garlic gum, garlic key chains, garlic body spray—they love it all. On top of that, he was a full-grown man wearing a high school class ring. I'd have to check, but twenty-to-one odds say that it was from a local public school.

My guess, the guy was a linebacker in high school, not good enough for college and for the last five or six years he's been doing the rounds of shitty jobs and blaming everyone but himself for his lot. This decade it's the vampire's turn.

I got off the bus on Fremont Street, the LED kaleidoscope of color assaulting me and making my head throb. Not long ago this whole strip was lined with colorful neon lights, but recent energy conservation laws forced some major changes. It wasn't a hard sell, twice as bright using half the energy. Everybody went twice as bright, much to my aching skull's discomfort.

The sign over the campaign headquarters read 'James Chandler for Congress.' From the street, I could see several college kids laughing and talking as they shuffled papers from one desk to another. A cute blond girl was flirting with a nerdy looking guy in a sweater-vest. A tall kid was carrying too many boxes from a back room and trying hard to make it look effortless. Several others were scattered throughout the office on phones and making calls. The door was open, and I walked through the bustle to within a couple steps of the back office before Sweater-vest stopped me.

"Can I help you?" he said sliding between me and the door. Something about the movement caught my attention. It was smooth, and he planted himself in a not quite casual stance, but he looked relaxed.

"Maybe," I said, and reached into my pocket for my phone.

I blame my cracked cranium for not seeing what was about to happen sooner.

Sweater-vest slid in close and pinned my arm to my chest in a move out of a Kung-Fu flick. One of the girls I thought was busy texting was behind me and holding a taser to my neck. A smaller girl appeared, as if from nowhere, behind Sweater-vest. She stood with that unmistakable stillness, her arms crossed.

"How about you just tell me," he said as if we were just having a normal conversation.

"I'm a private detective looking for someone who may have worked on this campaign," I said, keeping my voice calm, despite how I felt.

"Do you have a weapon in there?" He asked, glancing down to where my hand was stuck inside my jacket.

"No weapons, just my phone."

He backed up a bit, released the pressure on my arm as the taser pressed harder into my neck. These guys were pros, every move practiced and timed to perfection. I took out my phone and showed him my license and badge.

With a nod, the taser was taken off my neck, and my phone was plucked from my hand.

"We'll just verify your license real quick. Would you like to take a seat?"

I wanted to refuse but sitting sounded like a good idea.

"He's good," taser girl said. She handed me back my device. "Thank you for understanding."

I was beginning to understand but scowled at her non-apology.

"Sorry Detective, the closer we get to the election the crazier things seem to get," Sweater-vest said.

I looked back to the front of the room where the volunteers were having a hard time getting back to work after the brief excitement. I noticed for the first time that across the ceiling above the door hung several directional sensors, the hypersensitive ones that would have detected any weapon or explosive I may have been carrying. I looked back to the little vampire girl who would have been able to sense if I meant to do any harm. I realized that by being half-concussed and unobservant, I was able to stumble my way past most of their security measures.

"I'm sorry too," I said. "I should have called before coming." I never call. It's easier to read people's reactions in person.

"So, how can we help?"

I opened the photo I took of Barbara and Laura's drawing. Sweater-vest's right eyebrow rose a fraction in recognition.

"You know them?"

"I do, Laura and Barbara Rice. They were here every night for months. They stopped showing six weeks ago, last Tuesday."

"That's oddly specific. Did something happen that night?"

"It was the night of the debate. They got into a big argument with each other. It was frightening." He looked sideways at the vampire watching us before continuing, "I reported it to Candidate Chandler when he got back, but he said not to worry. I made note of it anyway."

"What did they fight about?"

"No idea," he said.

"It was a lover's quarrel," vampire girl said. Her accent was thick, Japanese or maybe Korean.

"Really?" I said, my full attention on her now.

"Laura was upset with Barbara's constant ..." she paused for the right word, "flirtations."

"There seems to be a lot of that going on here."

"It's normal for a campaign," Sweater-vest said. "Lots of young people working long hours for a like cause. I've seen places get hedonistic. Chandler keeps this place very conservative by comparison."

"Did that include Laura?"

He looked to the vampire.

"*We* all noticed." The way she said 'we' created a distinction. The vampires noticed. "It was apparent that one of them wanted to be a part of this campaign. After a month Barbara began charming all the men around her."

"After the argument?"

"They never came back," Sweater-vest said.

I took a deep breath, wished my head would stop throbbing, and tried to remove all accusation from my voice. "With this level of security, I'm guessing threats have been made against your campaign. Then a couple of your regulars disappear. You don't see any possible correlation?"

"No, not at all. The truth is, it's not that uncommon. Volunteers come and go from campaigns all the time. I assumed those two were too embarrassed to come back or that Chandler asked them not to."

"Can I speak to Mr. Chandler?"

"He's at a fundraising dinner. He won't be in tonight."

"Tomorrow?" I asked, wanting to rub the back of my head.

"I'll ask his assistant to contact you."

I know a dismissal when I hear one and made for the door. Sweater-vest walked me there.

"Hey, if you have any more questions, just give me a call."

When we reached the door, I pointed at the sensors and nodded at the rest of the security team. "Is all of this security necessary?"

"Seriously?" When he realized that I wasn't making a joke, he said, "James Chandler is going to be the first Vampire elected to the House of Representatives."

Three

Heading back to the bus stop I admitted that it wouldn't hurt me to read a headline from time to time.

"Detective Cain."

The voice was close as if whispered in my ear. I spun around, startled, and saw the young vampire from the future congressman's security detail.

"Do you have a moment to speak with me?" Although she was five yards away, her voice still sounded like a whisper in my ear.

I repressed a shiver and put on the most charming smile I could muster. "Of course, Miss …"

"I'm Kim Seo-yun."

"Okay Kim, did you want to tell me something about Laura and Barbara?"

The vampire stared at me long past the point of comfort before saying, "You said you were looking for someone, not that you were looking for a couple. Who are you looking for?"

"Barbara. Laura has asked me to find Barbara for her."

Another long silence but this one I broke.

"Okay Kim, I'm going to—"

She was on me. In a blink, my arm was in a vice grip, and I was pulled down, so we were face to face.

"First," she said in the same calm tone, "my family name is Kim. So, you should call me Ms.

Kim. Second, you need to stop thinking of vampires as the children some of us resemble. I am not a child that you need to patronize. I have lived your lifespan several times over."

I managed to nod my head to signal my understanding and hoped that my knees did not give out.

Ms. Kim released my arm and stepped away.

When my voice came back, I said, "I'm sorry. I didn't mean to be rude."

My hands were still shaking, so I shoved them deep into my coat pockets.

"You should also realize that we are simultaneously like and unlike other people. When we reach a certain age, we can lose connections with parts of our humanity. Whether it was from deeds or isolation, sometimes we no longer think or act the way you would expect. Your intentions are pure, you want to help your client, and that is very honorable," she said, her eyes never leaving mine even when I decided to focus on the cracks in the concrete. "I suggest you abandon this case."

She caught me off guard. I was expecting a threat, a warning to keep this matter away from her candidate, or maybe even an ultimatum. Ms. Kim, however, was warning me and doing it because of some kind of honor she could sense in me. I didn't know about any honor, it was a job I said I would do.

Her eyes bore into me. I nodded to the cracks on the ground and saw her turn to leave.

"Do you know where Barbara is?" I asked. I was glad my voice sounded more confident than I felt.

Ms. Kim turned to stare at me again. It wasn't easy, but I met her gaze and held it.

The slightest hint of a smile touched the corner of her mouth. "Ask around at the Eighteenth Century after two o'clock."

"Thank you," I said, shocked by her response.

"Your desire to understand us is admirable," she said, "but stupid."

Then she was gone, faster than I could see, and without a sound.

Four

I had hours to kill before two a.m., so I ducked into a coffee shop, ordered a triple shot of espresso, and from a table I wished was more private made a call to an old friend.

"Tito, how are you?" I said loud enough to annoy the purple-haired teens in the designer clothes at the next table.

"Your ears must be burning," Miguel said. His whisper was a sharp contrast to my greeting. "Where are you right now?"

"In a coffee shop on Fourth and Bridger."

"I'm close. Wait there for me." He hung up.

I asked the kids next to me for aspirin, and to my surprise, one girl opened a bag full of enough prescription drugs to fill a pharmacy. Not one to dabble in opioids, I declined.

"I have Midol," another girl said, and to my surprise, innocent giggles burst from the group.

I took the Midol with a big swig of my coffee.

"You're a godsend," I said.

That got me eye rolls and cold shoulders. I sipped my coffee and waited.

Miguel and I grew up together. Our fathers were partners, and our moms passed us back and forth depending on work schedules. We started boxing at the same gym, went to the same community college, and joined the police force together. We are brothers in all but blood.

When I quit the police department after my parents' death, we drifted apart. I burned a lot of bridges when I left the force but could always count on Miguel to pass me some info or run down the occasional address when I was in a pinch.

The girls took notice when he arrived. Miguel was tall and handsome, wearing a fitted shirt that showed off his physique. However, I think it was the police badge he wore around his neck that got their attention.

"Can I steal this chair?" he said.

Backs arched, and purple hair flipped. Of course, it was the badge.

"It's been a while," I said as he slid his chair close to my table.

"What the hell are you doing?" he said.

"I'm on a case," I said, confused by his aggression.

"I got a call from Captain Perez telling me that I needed to rein you in. Whatever case you're working on is done."

"Sure, no problem," I said.

Miguel laughed and shook his head. He knew me too well.

"Did you really take a case to find a missing vampire?" he asked, his voice a whisper again.

"Yeah."

Another laugh and shake of his head.

"Why does the brass care about a missing vampire?" I asked.

"One of James Chandler's lawyers called and said that you were causing a scene at their campaign headquarters."

"I left there less than an hour ago." I was amazed by the connections and the speed of the Chandler Campaign. I reached up to rub the back of my head but the lump there was still too tender to touch.

"What happened to your head?" Miguel asked.

"You're not the first person to tell me to drop the case. Hell, you're not even the second."

I gave him the rundown of the night's events ending with me showing him the portrait of Laura and Barbara.

"I don't know any vampires. It's not my department," he said, "but maybe we can find the guys who jumped you."

"The guy was wearing a high school class ring with a big ram's head on it. Do you remember what local school has a ram for a mascot?"

"No, high school was too long ago," he said pulling out his phone to do a search of local schools.

"R.H.S.," one of the teen girls said, not bothering to hide that she'd been listening.

"I blame reality television for the degradation of personal privacy," I said to Miguel.

He ignored me and turned on his most charming smile. "R.H.S.?"

All the girls answered, somehow without talking over each other.

"Rancho High School."

"The Rancho Rams."

"Next to Woodlawn Cemetery."

"Do you ladies go to Rancho High?" Miguel asked.

"No way."

"We go to the Academy."

"That's the high school for gifted artists."

"You wouldn't happen to know a former linebacker who was a big fan of gangster movies, would you?" I asked.

The girls gave me another synchronized eye roll.

Five

Outside, Miguel's unmarked car was parked in a tow-away zone. His partner, whose name I could never remember, was sitting on the hood of the car playing on his phone. When he saw me, he rolled his eyes in a manner reminiscent of my coffee shop fan club.

"Looks like my reputation with the force hasn't improved," I said to Miguel as he pulled a hefty laptop from his car and began to enter the vague description of my assailant.

"Nah, Chris is just a dick," Miguel said and smiled when Chris flipped him the bird.

I checked the lack of polish on my shoes to avoid looking in Chris's direction.

"Mom would like you to come by for dinner sometime," Miguel said, still focused on the computer.

"I'll call her."

"This weekend Sarah and I will be going. You should join us."

I nodded and raised my eyebrows in what I hoped was a convincing look of enthusiasm. Miguel didn't look like he bought it and was about to say so when a series of beeps came from the computer.

"This looks promising," he said, "Edward Stompanato, twenty-one years old, six-foot-one, and two-hundred-sixty pounds. He was picked up twice over the last year for aggravated assault, both times a Rancho High School ring was among his possessions."

"Can you give me his address?" I asked. I caught Chris taking interest from the corner of my eye.

"No," Miguel said, "I can tell you that both times he was pinched at Atomic Liquors."

"I thought that place was for tourists."

"It comes and goes," Chis said, then went back to Potato Paratroopers or whatever game he was playing.

"It's a couple blocks away," Miguel said, "Hop in, we'll check it out."

"Do you feel like cracking some heads?" I asked.

Miguel winced, and Chris looked at me like I was the village idiot.

"We're not cracking heads," Miguel said, "but if you can identify this guy as your assailant, we'll make the arrest."

"Nah, I don't want to press charges."

"You sure?"

"Yea, turn the other cheek and all that."

"Right," Miguel said, skepticism heavy in his voice. "You're also dropping the vampire case?"

"Oh yeah," I said, "It's not worth the trouble."

He didn't buy it, but Miguel embraced me in a brotherly hug, and I promised to call more often. Chris ignored me and slid into the car without saying a word. They drove off, and I started walking. My head was starting to feel better, so I gave a little wave of thanks as I passed the coffee shop window.

Atomic Liquors was a faux lounge with a cheesy 1960's theme. The smell of spilled beer and fried food hung heavy in the thick air. A dark wood bar with a mirrored back ran the length of the place. Most of the three-legged stools were empty, but along the back wall, the high-backed booths were full of kids trying to out 'Rat Pack' each other.

I walked close to the tables and made eye contact with everyone. I didn't know what this guy looked like. Miguel wouldn't show me his picture because he was afraid it would invalidate a future lineup. So, I stared down everyone at each table getting a mix of uncomfortable glances and more eye rolls. Until I came to the fourth table.

There were five of them seated boy-girl in the half-circle booth. I saw the look of recognition from one of the guys on the end. His eyes went wide as I stopped in front of his table. Edward Stompanato was sitting in the back, nuzzling the neck of the bottle-blond next to him. He looked bigger than I remembered, and I had a moment where I questioned my course of action.

"Stomp, it's the mark," the guy who recognized me said.

"Hey Eddie," I said as if we were best buds meeting by surprise. "You got a minute?"

Edward was slow to react, and I felt my odds improving.

The kid to my left made to get out of the booth.

Now, I'm no south-paw but my left hook is formidable, and my aim is impeccable. I tapped the kid on that little magic spot on a person's jaw, the one that makes the lights go out, and his head dropped to the table like he decided to take a nap.

I pointed at the guy on the other end, and he sat back in his seat. The girls were wide-eyed and too shocked to scream. Eddie focused on me, and I recognized his eyes.

"So, Eddie, who hired you to threaten me?"

Eddie grabbed the edge of the table and made a move as if he were going to flip it over on me. The table didn't move. It was bolted to the ground. He tried again, and a couple of the beer bottles on the table rattled but didn't fall. I was about to start laughing at him when he went into a rage.

He roared as he jerked the table up and down, the metal bolts creaking with every violent thrust. When the bottles fell over the girls began to scream. The guy I knocked out fell to the ground. His buddy dove the other way and made for the door. I slid my jacket off and tossed it on a barstool as I backed away.

This may not have been my best plan. Eddie was three inches taller, seventy pounds heavier, and guessing by his size and anger, he was juicing. When the table flipped I was already half a dozen steps back, hands up and ready to fight. He rushed toward me and by some stroke of luck slipped on the puddle of beer and broken glass.

I didn't hesitate for a second. I rained punches on him as fast as I could. Right hook to the temple, overhand left to the back of the neck, I stomped on his hand as he tried to get up and threw an uppercut to his face. I felt his zygomatic arch break with that last hit, but he was still struggling to get up. I moved down his back squatting low and working his body like a heavy bag. Rib, rib, rib, and then kidney. His back arched with that last one and he fell belly down on the ground.

I bounced back a couple steps, light on my toes and invincible.

I felt and heard the explosion in my head at the same time. Black spots began to burst at the corners of my vision. I turned and saw the brunette holding a broken bottle neck in her hand. Then I was out.

I woke up in an ambulance behind Atomic Liquors. A paramedic was shining the world's brightest penlight in my eyes. Miguel was standing over his shoulder, a grin spread across his face.

Of course, Miguel and Chris followed me, and when the bartender called the police, they were the first on the scene. They walked in to find me, Eddie, and Eddie's buddy piled up in a pool of beer, the girls screaming and brandishing bottles. In another stroke of luck, the security camera was positioned at just enough of an angle to miss my first punch, so it looked like I walked to the table,

Eddie flipped out and attacked me. With his history in the place and my friend on the force, I watched as the police hauled Eddie off to jail.

"Tell it to me straight Doc. Will I survive?"

"Could it improve his common sense?" Miguel said.

"Head trauma is nothing to joke about, Detective," the paramedic said, "You have one hell of a bump, the skin's not broken, but I think you should get scanned to see if you have a skull fracture."

"Any chance you could hook me up with some Advil and send me on my way?"

"Careful," Miguel said, "I may have to take you in for drug seeking behavior."

"Are you on any drugs now?"

"I took some Midol."

The paramedic stared at me for a long time trying to decide if I was joking.

I shrugged.

He gave me an ice pack, a small bottle of Tylenol, and told me to get my head checked.

"I've been telling you that for years," Miguel said as I reveled in the numbing sensation the icepack created. "You done with this now?"

"Yeah."

"Do you want a ride?"

"No, I need to get my jacket and some food," I said and gestured to the bar.

"Okay," Miguel said, resignation in his voice. "Don't forget dinner on Saturday."

I told him I'd be there and gave a polite wave to Chris, who ignored me.

Atomic Liquors looked the same as when I first walked in. The mess was cleaned up and the table repaired. My jacket was still laying across the bar stool, so I sat and ordered a burger, fries, and a coke, standard bar fare that is hard to screw up. My hands were filthy, so I went to the men's room to clean up. That's where I ran into Eddie's skittish friend, the one who bolted before all the action.

When he saw me walk into the bathroom his eyes bugged and he tried to squeeze past me out the door. A quick kick to his back foot as he raced past sent him headfirst into the porcelain tiled walls. Before he could get his wits about him, I flipped him over and put a knee on his chest.

"Hey buddy, I'm glad you decided to stick around."

"What do you want?" He was on the verge of tears.

"Who hired you and your friends to scare me off the case?"

"I don't know, man. I don't know. It was Eddie's deal."

"Tell me what you do know." I shifted my weight increasing the pressure on his chest. The guy didn't fight. He wheezed a little and gasped. I could tell that this was not a new experience for him.

"We just tail the fanger bitch and report what she's doing. When she went to your office, we were told to make sure you stayed away from her."

"Who told you? Who do you report to?"

"I don't know. Eddie handles all that."

"You have no idea?"

"Eddie checks in at that Vamp for President Place all the time, but I don't know who he talks to. Billy and I always wait in the car."

"Do you mean James Chandler's campaign office?"

"Yeah, that place or the Eighteenth Century."

Six

At two in the morning, I went to my first vampire club. I told myself I had never been to one before because I quit the club scene when I turned thirty, but if I'm being honest, they scare the crap out of me. I think most people have a curious fascination with them, like sharks or S&M. By law, none of them are allowed to be exclusive. In practice, people who go to places like that are all fang-bangers and wannabes.

Eighteenth Century was famous for its exclusivity. Located in a basement level of the vampire owned, Topkapi Saray Hotel and Casino, it's rumored the design is an exact replica of the Imperial Harem as it was during the reign of the Ottoman Emperor, Mahmud I. It displayed an Italian-inspired, Ottoman/Baroque that overlaid an ancient Ottoman architecture foundation, or so the advertisement in the elevator said.

The ad undersold.

The doors opened, and I stepped onto a courtyard at mid-day. The sky was blue, a cool breeze full of spice blew past me, and there was a band playing a melodic song on an open-air stage. Narrow alleys branched off the main square where vampires milled around in groups of three and four. No one gave me a second look. Somehow that put me even more on edge than if they stared.

The bar was set between two rooms decorated with colorful pillows and sheer silk drapery hanging from the ceiling. The bartender was adding a celery stick to a Bloody Mary when I approached.

"What can I get you?" he asked, not a hint of surprise or hostility in his voice.

"I was told I could find someone here."

"Sure, who are you looking for?" he said, again, like the nicest bartender on the planet.

I pulled out my phone and showed him the portrait.

"Oh, Barbara, she's usually down the south-east corridor." The bartender gestured to the alley to the right of the square. "Head down that way keeping right till the tiles turn red then check out the rooms on your left."

I said thanks to the Rockwellian bartender and headed in the direction he suggested.

The alley was narrow. I walked through mosaic tiled chambers and branching hallways. The tiles changed from green to blue to gold. Less than half the rooms I passed were occupied with men smoking long pipes, musicians playing beautiful music, or casual dinner scenes. There was laughter and song, and overall merriment, and I couldn't help but think it was all for my benefit.

Everyone I came across seemed to pay me little or no attention, but every time I passed an open room or a wondering group, the hair on the back of my neck would stand on end. The first couple times, it took considerable effort not duck or spin around to see where the attack was going to come from. Instead, I continued walking a few steps, turned as if to admire the artistry of the walls, and found that I was alone.

As I progressed, the sky grew darker. It took me less than five minutes to get to the red-tiled section, but the long shadows made it appear to be late afternoon or early evening. I stopped and looked up, in awe of the realism, not able to fathom the magic or technology that was used to create such a replica.

"Sad thing is," a deep voice said into my ear.

I screamed and jumped away from an old man who was gazing at the sky in the same way.

"Most of us just see the brush strokes," he said before turning and walking away.

I rubbed my face and ran my hands through my hair wincing when fingers touched the bump on my head. I told myself that I had not sounded like a nine-year-old boy on a carnival ride and that I was a tough-as-nails detective. Once that was established, I began checking all the doors on the left.

The first was closed. I approached it and could hear heavy breathing and moans. I couldn't tell if they were sounds of passion or pain, so I moved on. I was focused on being a tough guy detective when I ran into a wall of a man in a well-tailored suit.

"Can I help you? he said, with the same nicest guy in the world tone as the bartender.

"I'm looking for Barbara Rice," I said and reached for my phone.

"I have a visitor?" a woman's voice said from inside the room. "Bobby, let him in."

Bobby looked as if letting me in was the last thing he wanted to do. Just about the time I was convinced he wasn't going to move, he stepped back, and I walked in.

The room was unlit, the only light was from the single window and the door that Bobby stepped back in front of. Dark red tapestries and rugs covered every inch. A large circular bed covered in pillows dominated the room. In the middle, looking like a porcelain figurine, sat Barbara Rice.

"Hi, Ms. Rice, I've been looking for you."

"Really?" she said. She tilted her head, a gesture that should have implied confusion but on her, it looked … not unnatural, but primal, inhuman.

"Laura hired me to find you."

"Why?" she said, drawing the single word out.

"She thought that something may have happened to you," I said. I heard the octave change in my voice and knew I was losing my tough detective mask.

"She knows where I am."

"I'm sure. It didn't take me long to …" I began, but Barbara's facial expression changed to one of surprise. She began crawling across the bed toward me, her eyes wild. It was so predatory that I was afraid if I took flight I would be hunted.

"Who are you?" she asked.

I stood head and shoulders over her, but my heart raced as she began circling me.

"I'm a private investigator."

"No. Who are you?"

"I'm Ray Cain."

She stopped somewhere behind me. I couldn't hear her. I couldn't hear anything but the distant music.

"The son of Thomas and Mary Cain?"

I was shocked into silence. My parents died years ago. Their names were in the papers, but no one would have remembered that.

The silence felt endless, so I took a deep breath and said, "Yes."

She threw me ten feet across the room. My body somersaulted in the air and landed hard in the middle of the bed. Barbara was on top of me the moment I landed, her legs straddled my hips, her hand on my throat pinning me down.

Then she sniffed me, and I lost it. I flailed, thrusting my hips, punching, and tearing at her hand but she didn't move. Her grip on my throat tightened, and I began to black out.

Bobby flew across the room and tackled the girl off me.

Oxygen filled my lungs, and I scrambled toward the door. My feet left the ground, and my body slammed into the wall. Barbara gripped my throat again, her face inches from mine. I saw Bobby's headless body across the room.

"Oh, you are perfect," she said. "I would not have known to even ask for you."

I grabbed her wrist with both my hands, lifted both feet to her torso and kicked as hard as I could. She released my throat and backed up a couple steps. I crawled toward the door but was snatched back up. Barbara brought my lips to hers, and she kissed me, biting my lip just enough for a drop of blood to form.

"This is love," she said and moved to lick the blood from my lip.

"Barbara," a man called from the doorway. There was command in that voice and Barbara froze, her tongue extended, about to touch the growing drop of blood.

Four men, dressed and built like poor Bobby, grabbed Barbara and hauled her off me. The second they touched her the fight was on, but the four large men restrained her. She kicked and screamed, her face distorting out of human proportions.

James Chandler entered the room. He said Barbara's name again, and she stopped screaming.

"Ms. Kim, please escort our guest out of the building," he said, and I was helped to my feet by the security officer from the campaign headquarters.

When I got out of the room, I made a mad dash for the exit.

Ms. Kim grabbed my coat and stopped me. "You can't run. You're bleeding. If you run, you will have half the club chasing after you."

I nodded and tried to get myself together.

"Are you ready?"

I put my bleeding lip into my mouth and nodded again.

I followed Ms. Kim back through the silent corridors. There was no music, no talking, the silence was deafening. Just my breath and footfall. When we got to the courtyard, it was packed. Every vampire in the place stared right at me. Hundreds of silent, statuesque creatures watching me leave.

Once I was out of the casino, I sat down on a bench near the cab stop and buried my face in my hands.

"I'm sorry we were late," Ms. Kim said.

"I don't understand."

"I knew you would not quit looking for Barbara, so I told you where to find her. I hoped to be here before you arrived, to prevent something like that from happening."

Seeing my confusion, Ms. Kim continued, "Some of us don't handle the change well. Sometimes fragile minds break and it's the love we have for the weak that keeps us from freeing those that most need it."

I still didn't get it, but I nodded like I did.

"Now that you have found Ms. Rice, your case is over. Will you need a ride home?"

"I would love one."

Seven

The limo dropped me at my building. I stopped into my office long enough to grab the one vampire deterrent I owned before I made my way back to the bus stop. Three buses and a half-mile walk later, I was at Laura's suburban paradise. I dry-swallowed some Tylenol before ringing her bell.

The door opened and Laura's voice invited me in.

The house was surprising in its blandness. It looked new and smelled of fresh paint. I walked into an unfurnished entry, across beige carpets and bare white walls. It felt like a model home that was used to show potential buyers the bare bones. Then I walked into the living room.

The twenty-foot wall that spanned both floors of the house was painted to depict a war between heaven and hell. It was done in a classical style, like Rubens with its dramatic flow and lighting but in such realism, Gustave Courbet would have been in awe.

Life-sized devils crawled from the ground, made more real by the lack of a drop cloth allowing the mural to look as if it was spreading across the floor a drip at a time. They crawled up a rock face to battle the angels that were descending from above, all full of light and anger. I was overwhelmed. The painting both captivated and frightened me. It was magnificent, a true work of art, the likes of which I had never seen.

"Michael's nose still isn't right," Laura said. She was wearing a sheer painter's smock and nothing else. Paint covered her hands, and there was a swipe of black across her forehead as if she wiped away sweat.

Vampires don't sweat. She was putting on a show for me, trying to seduce me, but I didn't know why.

"I found Barbara."

Laura stopped, her head tilted. It was like the look Barbara gave me, just before she tried to eat me.

I did not look away.

"She's at the Eighteenth Century. Ask the bartender, he'll point you to the right room."

"You saw her?" Laura asked.

"I had quite the chat with her."

Laura's eyes went wide. It was not the answer she expected.

"I'm just here to collect the rest of my payment."

Laura walked across the room with a distracted look on her face. She tapped a couple buttons on her phone, and I felt mine vibrate.

"Great doing business with you," I said and turned for the door.

My hand was on the doorknob. I knew that I should just chalk this up as a win and leave. I went back to the living room where Laura was still standing with her phone in hand. I turned my back to the mural to avoid the distraction.

"You persuaded Barbara to join the campaign, not the other way around," I said.

"She hated it."

"It was James Chandler who convinced you to join."

Laura nodded.

"He wanted to keep you close. He was keeping an eye on you, had you followed. He was afraid of you hurting his campaign," I said. "He's the vampire that made you."

Laura's silence spoke volumes. Candidate Chandler couldn't have a psychopath daughter running around breaking the new laws. It would ruin his whole campaign.

"She began to act out, put the old vampire whammy on a few of the volunteers, and you guys fought," I said, trailing my words, hoping she would pick up the thread.

"She chose to go with James after the fight," Laura said. "You're right, he is the one who turned us, made us what we are. I thought we were free of his control after all this time. I thought we could be equals, family, something, but his control over us is strong, and he offered her the life she wanted."

"You weren't invited?"

"We freed ourselves from him over a hundred years ago. When our other sister was killed, James felt nothing. He did not weep. He did not seek revenge. I saw then what we were to him and I swore that I would never be his bride again."

"There is something I'm still missing here. Why did you hire me?"

"I miss her. I can't be without her anymore. I needed to win her back," Laura said. "You were going to bring her back to me."

"There are hundreds of investigators around town. Why did you choose me?"

Laura was silent and still.

"You were the perfect gift," Barbara said, from the loft behind me.

I jumped and saw that Laura was just as surprised.

In a blink of an eye, the two of them were in a lovers' embrace in front of me.

"You know me better than anyone," Barbara said.

"When he showed up here, I thought you rejected him, and me."

"Never again, my love."

I did not hesitate. I turned and ran only to be stopped by Barbara.

I threw a left-right combo, but nothing connected. She pushed my chest, and I went sprawling between them.

"Why me?" I asked again, still not understanding what role I played in this.

"Because your blood sings to me," Barbara said. They did not rush to get to me. They were taking their time, reveling in the moment. I began to feel an attraction to them that contradicted the fear that overwhelmed me. I needed to focus and keep them talking until I could figure my way out.

"How did you know my parents?" I said.

Barbara smiled, and it was frightening on her innocent face.

"Even before the coming out," Laura said, "things were different. We were forced to stop feeding on people. To become a part of society, we sacrificed what we are. We hunted our own kind who broke the rule, put them on trial, and executed them for doing what is in our nature."

"Some things in nature cannot be stopped," Barbara said. "Your father and mother got into an argument at that police bar near your old home, and your mother stormed out. Your father caught up to her at the canal overpass. He wrapped her up in his arms and begged for forgiveness your mother kissed him and begged him to forgive her. Their emotions were so strong, and their blood so enticing."

An overwhelming feeling of love and desire came over me as my gut sank and I realized where this story was going.

"I drained your mother as your father still held her in his arms. He watched as she died. I tossed her body into the canal as he attacked me. I let him hit me until he was exhausted, then I took his exquisite blood, and tossed him down to where your mother lay," Barbara said, a wistful look coming into her face. "They were the last humans I ever killed."

"The headlines read, 'Cop Kills Wife Before Taking His Own Life,' and the investigation was open and shut," Laura said. "Barbra was never suspected, even by our own kind."

I was dizzy. My emotions and those of the vampires collided and I was overwhelmed. I realized that although I touted it for years, I did not fully believe my father's innocence until that moment. The sorrow I felt for that betrayal was burned away by my anger. I was furious for what they did to me, to my parents, to my whole life.

I got to one knee, put my hand in my pocket, and wrapped my mother's old rosary around my knuckles. With every bit of speed and power I had, I threw an uppercut from the ground to Barbara's face.

She saw it coming and smiled in anticipation of a frivolous attack.

When I connected, however, her face broke open. From her jaw, through her chubby cheek, and across her little nose a piece of skin and flesh tore off and flew across the room. Black blood oozed down her face.

Her scream was instant and deafening. She fell to her knees and Laura went to her aid.

I ran for the door.

Laura grabbed me and forced me against the wall. I reached up and pressed the rosary to her face. Smoke rose from between my fingers as if I burned her, but I felt no heat. She screamed and struck my hand away with so much force I felt my wrist crack.

Laura's left eye was milky white, the contrast emphasized by the charred black skin that now covered a quarter of her face. She shoved away from me, and my head bounced off the wall.

I'd taken some hits in my day but nothing like that. It was the most excruciating pain I ever felt. My equilibrium disappeared, and I fell to my knees. I tasted bile in the back of my throat, and I felt my diaphragm convulse. I tried to look around but was unable to focus my eyes. I tried to crawl away, but my right hand wouldn't support me, and I ended up face down on the beige carpet with my ass in the air.

Barbara crawled into my line of sight. Her torn face was still dripping dark blood. "I will keep you alive for years, feeding on you every night. I will make you relive your parents' deaths over and over for the rest of your pitiable life."

She moved toward me in that predatory way. Her mouth opened, and I felt a breath on my neck and a drop of her blood land on my cheek before she sank her fangs into my throat. I felt a pop as the skin broke then all my pain vanished. I felt desire, and hunger, and anger, and love before Barbara was thrown off me.

Ms. Kim Seo-yun stood over me with a sword in her hand. "You were warned, Barbara."

"To hell with your warnings. I'm done with James and this society bullshit," Barbara said, that evil smile growing across her face, "and I'm done with you, executioner."

Laura came from behind and swept Ms. Kim's legs out from under her. The moment she hit the ground Barbara pounced. I heard snarling, mixed with cries of pain and anger. It was bestial, like wild animals fighting. Their movements were too fast for me to follow, but I had enough sense to start toward the door.

I made it to the hall before a hand as strong as a vice crushed my ankle. It was my turn to scream.

Barbara dragged me back into the living room and tossed me in front of the mural. Ms. Kim was being held by Laura, who was forcing her to watch. Her sword lay useless on the ground in front of her.

I held up my trembling hand to show the rosary. My wrist was swollen, and the beads dug into my skin.

"That is not enough of a deterrent for me. You have hit me with your best shot, and I'm still here."

She was right. There was no more fight in me, I was exhausted, and I couldn't go another round. I looked over at Ms. Kim. Her face was clawed, and bite marks ran along her arms, but she still struggled against Laura's hold. I began to unravel the rosary from my hand. As I did, I could feel Barbara's emotions taking over my own. I wanted her to bite me again.

"You are already mine," Barbara said.

"Yeah," I said. I balled the rosary in my left hand and yelled, "Duck."

I'm not a southpaw, but the rosary flew straight enough.

Laura ducked and Ms. Kim dove. She came up with her sword in hand, and in a move Zatoichi would have been proud of, she cut Barbara's head clean off.

Laura stood, awestruck. Ms. Kim took advantage and severed her head as well.

She stood staring at the bodies for a moment before saying, "It's almost dawn. I must leave." She rolled her shoulders and straightened her back before looking at me. Indecision crossed her face, and I would have sworn it was an honest emotional reaction. "Will you be alright?"

Sitting on my heels, unable to focus my eyes I said, "Oh, yeah. Don't worry about me."

Ms. Kim nodded and in a blink was gone.

Eight

I don't remember calling Miguel from Laura's house, but whatever I said convinced him to come en force. SWAT team, medical helicopter, and a dozen beat cops I would have sworn hated me arrived just after sun-up. My first ride in a helicopter, and I was unconscious the whole time.

I woke up a week later with a great tan. It turns out Vampires have this kind of venom that needs to work its way out of a person's system, and prolonged exposure to the sun helps speed the process. The doctor said that, with my severe head trauma, broken wrist and ankle, and a vampire bite, I was lucky to have ever regained consciousness.

When I was able to speak in complete sentences, I told Miguel about my parents. Later that week they exhumed their bodies. Knowing now what to look for, the medical examiner determined that they were bitten by a vampire. The loss of blood, which was once thought to have been washed away in the canal, was now recorded as a vampire feeding on them. My father's shattered knuckles, once thought to have been my mother's cause of death, were now recognized as a husband defending his wife.

It was over a month before I was back in my office but that first day I found out my father's life insurance policy and pension benefits were restored. Overnight, I went from being a deadbeat to a fat cat. I spent the majority of that day trying to figure out what to do with my newfound wealth.

At five past sunset that evening, I was reading a novel that took place in Chicago and considered taking a vacation there, when I got a knock at my door.

"Come in," I said and tossed my paperback into a desk drawer.

"It's good to see you back at work Detective Cain," Kim Seo-yun said as she entered my office.

"Ms. Kim, congratulations on your victory. I heard James Chandler won in a landslide."

"Thank you. James is a good leader and an honorable man. He was a great ruler long ago and he will be again."

That last put a little shiver down my spine.

"I should also thank you," I said. "You know, for saving my life and all."

"You saved mine as well. I did not expect that. So, my thanks to you. I believe we are even on that count."

I didn't think we were anywhere close to being even. I owed her my life but having just freed myself from that debt I decided not to argue.

"So, is there someone else James wants me to stay away from?" I said. "Believe me, I'm willing to listen this time."

Ms. Kim laughed.

It was an amazing sound, full of life and energy. It made her look even younger.

"No," she said, "My contract with James Chandler was for the duration of the campaign."

"Oh, did you come here just to visit me?" I thought I saw a moment of hesitation.

"No," she said, "I have a new client, and I would like your assistance."

I said I was done working with vampires. It wasn't worth the pain. I almost didn't make it out of the last case alive. Heck, I still hadn't fully recovered, I was sitting at my desk with braces on my ankle and wrist. It was ridiculous to think that I would be interested in pursuing another case involving vampires.

Of course, if I really meant to avoid these kinds of cases, I would have closed my office before the sun went down.

"Do you need me to find another missing vampire?" I said and smiled.

Ms. Kim shook her head and smiled back at me before asking, "What do you know about werewolves?"

Coming Out of The Coffin

R. S. Pyne

My phone rang at three in the afternoon on the Day of Revelation—never a good time to get a call. Whatever I drank last night did not agree with me. The hangover demons banged around my skull and roared; old enough to know better but why change the habits of a second lifetime? Nausea put in an appearance, second-hand synthetic oblivion lingering still.

"Turn your screen on," the voice ordered, not the kind of voice you ignored if you wanted to continue to exist. "Any channel, doesn't matter … he's on all of them."

I switched the infernal machine on and felt worse. She looked so clean and wholesome, a pretty college girl and head cheerleader with 'bite-me' eyes. Rude not to oblige; alone at the bar, she hunted for someone to offer her a drink, not far from my own reasons for being there. Now, her blood tasted sour and tainted.

"We should have dealt with Smith before he became a problem … before he went public."

A short, ratty object stared at the camera, specially developed equipment with Nosferatu filters to capture his image and transmit it to the watching world. Vlad Smith blinked in the limelight, windows in his interview room specially sealed, so no sunlight spoilt his moment. Not much to look at—a dirty little secret on a minor league player's conversion list. Nobody had ever heard of him before he called a press conference and sent our world spiraling down the toilet. We were not ready to come out of the coffin.

"It is on every social media feed," the voice informed me. "Every channel, streamed live across the globe."

The shock of the revelation that we existed would surprise the seven million vampires who already knew.

"His sire has been located and … sanctioned."

A polite, watered down euphemism; we both knew what that meant. He did not need to spell it out. William Augustine could have ordered his turning to keep silent, using a master's power of veto to ensure revelation never happened. For some reason, he chose not to interfere.

"We are in your communities, in your schools and hospitals; your universities and nursing homes

… your next-door neighbors, work colleagues and friends. We hide what we are because it has always been that way, from the beginning. My kind walked on the Earth first, but we have shared it with you, hidden in plain sight." Vlad read from an autocue, stumbling over the words. "Not anymore. It is time to stop hiding."

He paused again for dramatic effect, panic on his face as a large, purple-haired woman broke through the security cordon, eggplant painted fingernails hooked for clawing.

Nobody human saw her true nature; she knew better than to give him any proof, her expansive bosom emblazoned with Christian propaganda.

My sister-in-fang, one of the few others of our dam's children to make it through the last Purge, screamed at Smith and called him a fantasist. She had been sent by The Council as damage control, careful to act human.

"This is how it started last time," the voice told me. "Three staking's on the first day, thirteen the following night, turned into thirty the day after that. Do you want me to do the math? The werewolves are worried it will set a precedent."

We had co-existed with humanity long enough to know that the thin veneer of civilization could be scraped off like old paint. Scratch the surface, and man got ugly—fast; mob-law applied.

"It is time to take our rightful place by your side." Vlad Smith opened his mouth and extended his fangs for the first time. One of the journalists fainted, the sound of her unconscious body thudding to the floor loud after the stunned hush. Up to that moment, everyone in that room still believed it to be a hoax, a stage-managed publicity stunt organized by a mediocre horror writer with a new book to sell.

"I want an equal partnership based on tolerance and trust."

The last time anyone tried that, it ended badly. Vampire-kind does not play well with others, and humans never share.

'Stop playing with your food,' my dam always said, in the early years after conversion when everything still felt new and exciting.

"We are not the enemy," Smith said, "We take only what we need to survive."

"Clean this mess up," the voice was imperious, used to giving orders and having them obeyed without question. "Show that the old rules still apply even if the world has changed."

No shit. I watched another woman throw herself onto the stage and claw Smith's face down to the bone, less discrete than my sister in fang; little more than a child with no master's guidance. Some people just could not cope with revelation, the sudden crashing end to their life in the shadows. This one was ugly enough to want to stay there, built like an all-in wrestler on a bad day. One of the security guards made a wild grab for her, but was too slow. She threw him across the room with contemptuous ease. An amateur's display, professional pride would never have allowed me to act in such a way or be seen undead in a bright orange kaftan, oversized dark glasses, and turquoise hair. Her short skirt left nothing to the imagination, but it should have tried a little harder.

"How do you want it done?" I already knew the elders needed something or why call? Wet-work, to send a clear message to show what happened to those indiscrete enough to reveal our secrets to a world that still believed in Santa Claus and the Easter Bunny.

My kind arrived first, evolving to specialize on the pre-hominid and hominid lines. We preyed on Australopithecus and Homo neanderthalis long before Homo sapiens. The real reason primitive humans discovered fire—to keep the things that lurked in the shadows at bay, or at least to see them coming.

There were no Ancients left to remember a time when we were the dominant species. The last of the First Ones died final death millennia ago, but for a moment, I felt their essence shout orders at me.

Vlad Smith continued his speech, as Orange Kaftan exploded. Quite literally blowing her top before security could reach her.

She threw Holy Water into Smith's face and swallowed the rest in a televised suicide. He looked shocked, sallow skin already beginning to bubble.

The blessed H_2O only burned if vamps believed it could.

Positive thinking and mindfulness made it non-corrosive, but Smith stepped back smoking as his would-be assassin melted into a pool of bloody slurry. The cameras captured it all, zooming in on reaction shots from the assembled journalists and stunned studio audience.

"We'll take a short commercial break now," the female presenter said, with a bright, maniac's smile frozen on her face. "Stay tuned viewers. Mr. Smith has agreed to answer questions."

After they cleaned up the mess and waited for his face to grow back.

"How quickly can you get across town? You will have a second on this one."

"Do I have a choice?" I came close to open rebellion as the hangover flared back, worse than ever.

"With respect," the addition did not make it any better, but the elder ignored my sarcasm, too grand even to register it.

"She is a new turn on her last warning. Her sire never bothered to show even the basics. It is a wonder she even made it this far. Get to the press conference."

He ordered me to deal with Smith, making it clear not to come back without the little man's head in a box. Zurich all over again—the reason why I usually did wet work gigs alone.

Nothing left to do but get moving. It would be impossible on human roads but easier by Blur. Not all vampires could move at four times the average human speed. Some did not have enough darkling energy to win a three-legged race with a five-minute head start.

"The novice will meet you at the studio … her name's Scarlett Vein."

Typical newbie mistake—the choice of name was always left to the convert, but only an idiot chose something they would be stuck with for centuries.

The city's underbelly, passages dug a hundred years earlier made daytime traveling easier, crowded now and everyone talking about the Revelation. Panic washed through the tunnel network, no time to stop even if small talk had been my favorite thing in the world. One of the Burnt Ones fell into step, wild-eyed crazies who still believed that sunshine and vampires mixed given enough faith and positive mental attitude.

Far above, the thoughts of the mortal and immortal world flowed, electric and easily tapped. The humans had been unprepared for the news that we existed.

My uninvited companion thought I gave a damn for his opinion. Once, he had been a high ranked elder, before he listened to the madness that comes from an overdose of centuries.

"They are just waiting for an excuse to wipe us all out."

His voice sounded like a cracked reed, eyes crimson in the half-light. "The city has been like a powder keg for years, set off by just one spark."

In the green room of a nondescript recording studio, the spark waited, perhaps sensing the council always had a backup plan.

Already news: a human mob had already killed two vampires and a homeless guy who just made the mistake of being in the wrong place. They called it self-defense, but that was how purges started in the old days. The panic came from both sides.

My brothers and sisters-in-fang woke early to find the world had changed, their fears counterbalanced by human terror—the sudden realization they were not alone, and the things in the shadows were real. That sort of panic caused ripples, impossible to smooth over, however much fake news the misinformation units released. Patterns had already shifted, with the eternal dance between prey and predator turned into a frenetic tarantella instead of an elegant waltz.

My mood had not lifted when I finally reached the studio's abandoned basement area that led up from the tunnels.

The girl waiting for me in the shadows did not look as if she wanted to dance; a slight tremor on one side of her face told me that; and the way she played with a stray lock of hair and pulled at the crimson elastic band around one slim wrist didn't bode well. Newness still shone brightly, too young to learn that immortality is a curse as well as a blessing. Two sides of the same coin—pain and pleasure decided on a single flip, too much of a child to know that sometimes fate used a two-headed penny.

Scarlett Vein acted tough, a kick-ass, hard-case bitch but I could see straight through the façade. A nastier vamp might have taken advantage, but we were on a tight deadline—make Smith dead by dusk or be dead ourselves. The Council ordered Scarlett to shadow me and learn the enforcer's trade because they didn't know what else to do with her. According to her files, she failed the compulsory after-life careers guidance three times, with the worst score in three human lifetimes: a case study of how not to do it.

"What do you want me to do?" she bared her fangs in an enthusiastic snarl, no idea that the Elders told me to give her a second death if she screwed up.

"Stay out of my way."

"There is no need to be like that." She shrugged as if she had abandoned any hope I would welcome her as a willing mentor. "They warned me you could be a little … prickly."

They probably said worse, but names never hurt anyone. A stake through the heart or a good old-fashioned beheading was always fatal, but no vampire ever died because someone called them mean. She pulled the elastic band again, as if that had all the answers, but it calmed her, helped her to meet my gaze. We wandered through each other's thoughts and compared scars. Enough for both of us, my long ago, barely remembered traumatic human childhood replaced by early years as a vampire in the worst purges since the Inquisition— no time for gentleness or patience.

"No wonder you are like that," she said, breaking contact because there was no more time for non-verbal small talk.

Searching for Smith's weasel-mind changed the subject. Concentration made her cross-eyed with the effort. He cringed in the green room, too stupid to run. He knew the Council would send a professional, the volunteers only an inconvenient diversion as he enjoyed the attention, the first time in his life—or afterlife—that anyone showed any interest. They flattered his ego, his fifteen minutes of fame magnified to two hours on all channels and exclusive interviews in every national newspaper. What happened afterward no longer mattered; he lived for the here and now and to hell with the consequences.

Scarlett raised her head, recalling a mind that did not practice enough to be a natural. My first solo-mind flight was three days after second-birth and all the way across the city; yet she found it difficult to travel two-hundred yards without breaking a sweat.

Minimal security, a few armed officers in the studio that kept a discrete distance—low-key surveillance experienced enough to stay out of camera shot, but they were human, with no special talents. They dealt with everyday human crazies and vampire nobodies, not prepared for what would come afterward. Scarlett would make them laugh; nobody ever took that kind of face seriously, a child-like quality in the eyes gave a weird vulnerability. She would remain a child forever, wide open and easy to read but still thought she was doing well.

"I can feel him squirm," she said in a hushed voice, sounding surprised. Did she expect me to hold her hand on the first job? She would either screw up and be ended or see Smith's second death. The elders needed a scape-bat, someone to blame if it went wrong so they could wash their hands of it. She did not know how to put mind-voice on silent or private; any vampire within a mile of this place could hear her.

Almost an embarrassment, if I cared enough to comment.

"He is at the end of the corridor, alone and isolated."

She did not have to add the fact that he drank alone with an untouched basket of complimentary fruit they gave to all guests and a perfectly chilled type O blood bag.

Ten minutes before they went on air again, last equipment checks and a less than dynamic duo of harassed runners who did not challenge our right to be there. No need for them to die—a pointless waste of resources to kill without need.

The politicians already called for a voluntary registration scheme, but they used a different word back in the day. We would be banned from the hunt, despite the fact that humans killed more of their own kind than vampires ever did.

Scarlett did not share my consideration, grabbing the college student by the arm and swinging him into a fatal embrace. Her fangs were in his neck, one manicured hand clamped over his mouth before he could scream. No choice but for me to take the other before he escaped to raise the alarm. Unlike her, I did not play with my food and he fainted in an ungainly heap on the floor.

"If you're not hungry, it seems a shame to waste him," her eyes were flush with blood and balefire. We did not have time for long drawn out self-indulgence.

She had never been through the Hungry Time when there were too many of us for the human population to maintain. Competition for prey drove many noble lines into extinction by their inability to change habits to suit a world that had moved on—adapt or die. What part of no did she have trouble with? I pushed her away from the senseless body, ignoring the sensual pulse of a rich vein so easy to tap. She yowled at me like an angry cat and only then remembered her manners, trying again when she thought my back was turned, but I moved too quickly for her.

"Let's get this over with," her voice was sulky, a petulant child being told not to do something. A good reminder of why I had no progeny. Never saw the need to bring more of my kind into existence, too busy with my second life to bother with anyone else's.

We were there to kill someone who exposed us all, not for an afternoon tea party. She twanged the rubber band and said I should try a similar technique for anger management. Showing her a fist-sized ball made from the bands did not stop her pestering.

"It didn't work for you, then?"

"What do you think?"

The surviving runner regained consciousness to see a violet-eyed, raven-haired killer dispose of his friend. In fact, he saw a pair of legs disappearing down the building's waste disposal chute. For such an ethereal thing, she had a large appetite, rarely sated for long and always looking for another victim. Something coursed through the kid's system, his eyes unfocused by more than terror. Could she not smell it? The scent of synthetic pleasure flooded every vein, every artery, the same residual dreck that caused my hangover; a lasting reminder of the girl I half drained and then left at the emergency room.

Scarlett snarled when I caught her by the wrist. One crimson painted hand slapped across my face, a hard blow followed by claws extended to scratch down to the bone. She still thought she could beat me in a fair fight, the natural optimism of a spoiled child.

"Will you sign the register, if it comes to that?" She changed the subject.

"No," memories of the last census returned, a bright scheme that seemed good at the time quickly turned into carnage on both sides. It gave me no hope for a workable solution.

Damn Smith and his publicity stunt. If the Elders did not order me to terminate him, I would have done the job myself.

"Just finish it." The dry, humorless voice of the First-among-Fangs Gerhard Jaeger intruded, arrogant, expecting instant obedience.

Scarlett abandoned all thoughts of a second victim; she focused, trying to at least appear competent, still under a death sentence if she made a mistake. The red band around her wrist, pale as chilled alabaster in the weak strip of light, mirrored the scars—telltale cross cuts. Injuries inflicted during our mortal lifetimes did not fade on conversion. They remained as permanent reminders that follow us into eternity; a popular misconception that the canvas is always wiped clean, made afresh and perfect—that would be too easy.

"I was in a dark place," she said, assuming I wanted an explanation but that was her business and nothing to do with me.

The only business we had in common, at this moment in time: to ensure an ending. Smith had already announced to the world that vampires were not fictional. His execution would send a clear message, a stark warning of what happened to anyone else who sold their story. Damage limitation, it also showed the power of our ruling elite. Even now they held all the top positions, their rank and status jealously guarded like gold in a vault and not inclined to share with lesser immortals.

For a brief mayfly moment, a treacherous thought crossed a mind that had been loyal far too long.

What would happen if we just let the whistleblower walk away?

I squashed the mutiny before it spread, before it could be used against me. Gerhard Jaeger had always been a patron—the maker of my own maker, and that gave him an automatic right to be obeyed in all things. To go against his direct order—an unthinkable impossibility.

Scarlett raised her head, a sing-song snarl in her voice, eyes glowing.

"He is trying to get out of the window."

The stink of burning flesh billowing from under the door told me that.

He had locked the door, only seconds left before the smoke alarms went off and the entire building evacuated. Three-thirty in the afternoon with the sun shining brightly outside spelled instant incineration if he chose that way out.

"Idiot," she smashed her way into the green room with one lady-like kick of her stiletto-heeled, designer boots. Smith stood there, his charred flesh trying to repair itself as all the raw nerve endings screamed at once. Looking at him reminded me of Prague and an ambush set by someone who called himself a friend. It took six months for the pain to stop. The target did not have that luxury and knew it.

Scarlett leapt on him, making the classic beginner's mistake. She moved in the way he expected her to move. Although Smith was the runt of an atrocious litter, he had existed long enough to know the tricks—an idiot, but a street smart one—all the self-interest of a gutter rat. He threw a table at her and snapped one of the cheap chairs to make a serviceable stake. His lips had been burned away, teeth pulled back from the blistered gums, only a shred of sinew and gristle holding his lower jaw in place until he pulled himself together.

"Nice try, girlie," he said, too stupid to recognize a diversion when it slapped him across the face. She distracted him long enough for me to go into shadow mode—one of the benefits of three hundred years of practice. Despite her newbie error, she did not deserve a second death, inexperience her only real failing. She deserved a chance. If the elders asked for an after-action report, they would hear only positive things.

"Did you come all this way to die alone?" Vlad Smith degenerated into a classic stereotypical villain, even his question clichéd and predictable as dawn followed dusk.

"No," she said, breaking his nose with a thoroughly modern headbutt he did not see coming. "I brought company."

He must have known she would never be trusted with a solo so soon after conversion, realizing too late that an enforcer followed close behind to get the job done. Scarlett turned his attention back to herself, drawing him on with a calculated insult nice girls were not supposed to know. He bared his fangs, seeing an easy target—a bully as well as a fool.

"The Council sends their regards," I said, flowing out of the shadow and back so he could not see which direction the attack would come from. Not much of a fighter, weak as ditchwater in the rain. Blur-rage filled me now, anger at what he had done to us all. It would have happened sooner or later as the world changed—might as well get it over with. All that remained was to take his head.

"Two minutes, Mr. Smith," one of the studio runners knocked at the shattered door frame. A projected glamor meant that he saw nothing wrong. "Two minutes to the Q&A session."

By that time, their star guest was no longer in any fit state to answer questions.

The dark thread linking all vampires past their first century throbbed, taut and close to breaking; some were terrified, but others were ready for war. Many of the younger vampires had been caught unprepared for Revelation. After the initial shock died down, we would be yesterday's news.

Mobs always found something else to riot about for that was in their nature. The older ones among us could easily adapt. We had all seen change before and no longer feared it.

Darkened Lives

Glen Damien Campbell

This is going to cause a problem, Clarice Daniels thought as, courtesy of her bedroom door being ajar, she overheard the faint particulars of the news report her mother was watching downstairs.

Despite her unease at what she was hearing, Clarice continued to get ready for her date, humming the melody of a Chopin prelude to herself and trying not to think about the nervous wreck downstairs, which, after hearing such momentous news, would be all that remained of her mother.

Unlike her mum, who had the social life of an anchorite, Clarice had no time to reflect on the day's breaking news, no matter how earth-shattering it was, she had a date to get ready for.

After much internal deliberation, she put the red halter-neck dress back in the closet. The racy dress, with its plunging neckline, had been Clarice's go-to outfit for many second dates; it had just the right ratio of vixen to virgin about it, which made it one of Clarice's most cherished and reliable outfits. And yet, despite now being in the process of getting ready for her big second date with Junji, who, in Clarice's opinion, had made himself more than worthy of seeing the sexy red dress tonight after making her keel over with laughter during their first date with a devilishly funny, self-effacing quip about his inability to grow facial hair, something in the pit of Clarice's stomach was telling her that skinny jeans and a blouse, conservative not sexy, was the way to go.

Maybe the news from downstairs is spooking me, she thought, as she buttoned up her red satin blouse. *Poor Junji, that news reader just lost you a night of staring down at my cleavage.* Clarice chuckled.

She zipped up her stone washed jeans and admired her tight, round ass in the Cheval mirror for a moment or two. When she was finished, she stepped across to her congested ten tier shoe rack and was just about to begin the painstaking process of deciding what shoes to wear when she heard her mother call.

"Clarice!"

As expected, the summons from downstairs had finally come.

"Yeah," Clarice shouted back, "what is it, Mum?"

"Can you come down here for a moment, please; I need to talk to you."

Ominously, Clarice could hear the anxiety in the timbre of her mother's voice. She rolled her eyes, sighed, and yelled, "I'll be down in a minute."

Too distracted now to pick out shoes with her usual thoughtfulness, Clarice hastily completed her outfit by randomly plucking a pair of ankle boots from the shoe rack, before going on to adorn her neck with a gold necklace bearing a crucifix pendant, which she took from among the more utilized treasures of her jewelry box.

When she arrived downstairs, Clarice found her mother in the living room, sitting on the settee, smoking a joint with a roach clip and encircled by a pungent haze of smoke. The stump of her truncated left leg, amputated at the knee, was perched on a footstool. Leaning up against the seat beside her was her detached prosthetic leg. As usual, she was staring at the TV screen, which, as no conventional lights were on, bathed the middle-aged woman with pale radiance. On the glass coffee table in front of her, next to a tin box chockfull of weed and rolling papers, was a glass of whiskey. Clarice was surprised to see that the bottle had not yet been brought in from the kitchen.

Without turning to look at Clarice, the woman in the ash-flecked housecoat said, "You're not going out tonight, are you?"

"I've got a date," Clarice answered.

At that, Clarice's mother shifted her body to look at her.

"A date," she probed, "who with?"

Clarice scoffed and shook her head in a way she hoped conveyed her incredulity at being asked that question.

"It's the same guy I went out with last Saturday," Clarice answered. "I told you all about him."

After looking confused for a second, Clarice's mother stared off into space and, for the moment, withdrew into herself as she tried to sift through her cerebral debris and find the memory of her daughter dishing-up details of her latest beau. To support her efforts, she brought the roach-clipped joint back up to her whiskey-moistened lips.

Like that's going to help your brain cells, Clarice thought, as she watched the tip of the joint glow bright yellow.

At that moment, as if sucking on the joint really was an aid to memory, Clarice's mother's eyes widened, surely indicating she had found the misplaced memory.

"The ginger Jap?" she said, presenting what she had dug up while exhaling dancing wreaths of cannabis smoke.

Close enough, Clarice thought, giving her head another little shake.

"His parents are Japanese," Clarice corrected, "he was born here. And he's not ginger, his name is Junji."

As Clarice spoke, her mum impatiently nodded her head as if to assert that she didn't need to be told these particulars again.

"I remember. I remember," she said, flapping her hand about dismissively. "You met him at that night class you're taking; Film Studies, or some such useless twaddle." She sucked her teeth loudly. "Anyway, it really doesn't matter who he is. What does matter, though, is that I'd rather you didn't go out tonight."

"Why?" Clarice asked, playing dumb, curious to see how her mother was going to break the big news.

"I just heard the damnedest thing on the news just now," she said. "You'll never believe it. It's going to change everything."

"I heard it from upstairs, Mum," Clarice confessed, unable to resist the perfect set-up to shock her mother with a blasé attitude. "I don't see what you're getting so worked up about, so the news is reporting that vampires are real, I don't see the big deal. Is it really going change things? It doesn't mean we're now going to have to cower away indoors every night after the sun goes down."

"Doesn't it?" Clarice's mother countered, fear, bordering on hysteria, was noticeable in her eyes. "I don't know, maybe I am overreacting," she continued. "But I just don't see any other way to react. It was on the news; vampires are real! Do you know what that means? Out there, tonight, there are individuals who look on us as prey. That's terrifying, and so I don't think it's safe to go out there, at least, not tonight, not on the night this news has broken."

Clarice, still finding pleasure in playing the unflappable youth, smirked.

"What, Mum, are you worried they're going to get me?" she said, waggling her fingers as she made a bogeyman pose and mocking her mother's concerns with her tone, which was saturated with sarcasm.

"Don't make fun of me, young lady; I'm just trying to look out for you."

"I know, I'm sorry, Mum," Clarice said, "but I'm going out tonight, whether you like it or not. But, if it makes you feel better," she reached into her blouse and hoisted out the gold crucifix, "I'll be wearing this. This should protect me, shouldn't it?"

From the street outside, a car horn sounded.

Clarice scampered across to the window, pulled back the curtains a smidgen and saw Junji's silver hatchback parked in front of the house.

"That's him," she announced, "I'm out of here."

"Please don't go out tonight, Clarice," her mother said, "I'll be worried sick if you do. I'll be pulling my hair out, I'll drink too much and then, who knows, I might do something crazy." As she spoke, with no subtlety at all, she pushed up the right sleeve of her housecoat and began pawing at the self-harm scars on her wrist. This, though, was an old ploy and Clarice had developed immunity to it.

Unmoved, Clarice calmly walked up to her mother and planted a kiss on her cold, sweaty forehead.

"Mum, I love you," she said, "but I'm not going to allow myself to end up like you. And, if you really love me, you wouldn't want me to."

The slap caught Clarice flush on her right cheek. Half expecting it, she took it stoically, resisting the compulsion to retaliate in kind, which was what her mother wanted; she wanted a fight. If Clarice had struck back like she used to, then her mother would have called her an 'ungrateful bitch' while stubbing out her joint on Clarice's arm, and then that would have really set things off. In an instant, they would have been on the floor brawling, clawing at each other's clothes and pulling each other's hair, like two women in a sleazy scene from a 'women in prison' exploitation movie. Of course, Clarice, younger, stronger and fully limbed, would eventually get the upper hand, ending the scuffle with a particularly lethal punch, or drawing blood with a bite. Guilt, though, would then disarm her and she would feel duty-bound to spend the rest of the night nursing her wounded, invalid mother.

Clarice would have won the physical tussle, but her mother, the masochistic manipulator, would have won the psychological one.

That was the scenario Clarice's mother had intended for them, but Clarice, now wise to all her mother's tricks, was determined not to play along.

"How dare you doubt that I love you," Clarice's mother said, in defense of her assault.

Junji's car horn sounded again.

"Christ, he's an impatient little fucker, isn't he?"

Without a word, again refusing to bite at the bait dangled in front of her, Clarice turned her back on her mother and began to walk away.

"Go on leave. Your Nip is waiting for you, you hussy. I was just trying to be a good mother, to protect you. But maybe I shouldn't care. Maybe, if those monsters out there get you, I should be happy; you'd no longer be a burden on my heart."

At the door, Clarice picked up her house keys from the console table and looked back at her mother.

"I'll be back before one," she said, using her words as an olive branch, and then, before her mother could say something to make her regret the concession, she walked out the door.

"Is everything okay?" Junji asked as soon as Clarice got into the car.

Straightaway, she realized what provoked his question. Unconsciously, she had been palming her sore right cheek, the cheek her mother had slapped.

"Yep, everything's fine," she answered, confining her hands to her lap. "So, what are we doing tonight?"

"I don't know, how does dinner and movie sound?"

"That sounds good to me," Clarice answered, "so long as it's not a vampire movie."

Junji laughed. She liked his laugh; uninhibited and genuine.

"So, you heard the big news," he said. "Crazy, isn't it? You know, I was worried you were going to cancel our date tonight because of it."

"Why would I do that?" she asked.

He shrugged. "I don't know. I guess maybe I thought you'd get jitters about going out after sunset."

She looked at him pointedly and said, "I'm not afraid of the dark, Junji."

"Not even now, when you know there are vampires lurking in it?"

"There were vampires lurking in it before I knew they were there," Clarice said, "and they didn't do me any harm, so why should they now."

"That makes sense," Junji appraised. "But, then again, maybe the real reason you're not afraid to come out at night is that, deep down, you want a sexy, long-haired, frilly shirt wearing vampire to come along and sink his teeth into you."

"Put me in the thrall of his hypnotic eyes," Clarice added, playing along, "dress me up in a sexy negligee, free me from my sexual inhibitions and make me his immortal bride?"

"Exactly, only you'll be in for a bit of a disappointment," Junji cautioned, "they're not immortal; they just age at a slower rate."

"Really?" Clarice said.

"Yeah, they age in a century what humans age in a decade and garlic doesn't harm them, that's bullshit, too. Oh, and a love bite on your neck isn't going to turn you into one; vampires are born, not made."

"Well, you certainly know a lot about them," Clarice said.

In response to this observation, Junji seemed to squirm in his seat as if she had just accused him of something.

"It's all anyone is talking about," he said, explaining away his apparent expertise. "I switched on the radio to hear the football scores and instead all I end up hearing are so-called vampire experts. I guess they must have learned a lot from that bloodsucker they caught."

"And dissected," Clarice added.

"Do you think that was wrong?" Junji asked.

Like she was trying to suck something out from between her teeth, Clarice scrunched up her mouth as she mulled over the question.

"You find something you don't understand," she said, "you take it apart to see how it works. It's what inquisitive people do?"

"I suppose," her date agreed, though she no longer had his complete attention. His eyes had veered away from Clarice, and he was looking past her. "Your mum," he said, "is she an inquisitive person?"

"Why do you ask that?"

"Because that's her watching us isn't it?"

Subtly, Junji gestured towards the house. Acting on his prompt, Clarice turned around, and sure enough, saw her mother at the living room window, holding the curtains back, watching them.

"Yeah, that's her," she admitted, flushing with embarrassment as she shrank back in her seat; women in their mid-twenties weren't meant to still have parents watching over them on dates. "Can we get out of here, please?"

Sympathetic to her embarrassment, Junji said nothing else until he had started the car and driven them away from the house with the prying eyes.

The movie they ended up seeing, Les Cauchemars Naissent la Nuit, an erotic thriller, was, in Clarice's opinion, turgid. It did though,

provide the two film students plenty to chew on over dinner, particularly as Junji, who had a taste for sleazy euro trash, proudly proclaiming Giallo and nunsploitation to be his two favorite genres, rather enjoyed it.

After leaving the restaurant, a quaint Italian place that had just served Clarice probably the second-best steak she had ever eaten, Junji suggested that they take a walk along the canal bank.

Though it was past midnight, and the promise to her mother hadn't been forgotten, Clarice agreed, sure that Junji was planning to kiss her at some point during the stroll. It would be their first kiss and the canal bank, Clarice had decided, was a suitably romantic place for it to occur.

"So, how long have you been looking after your mother?" Junji asked as they strolled along the paved towpath.

The question was the product of an awkward silence. In anticipation of Junji's kiss, Clarice had become taciturn, not wanting a drawn-out discussion about something to distract her man from his goal.

Junji though, seemed to find the silences that would occur after each one of Clarice's brief responses uncomfortable and so would quickly try to get the conversation flowing again, like it had in the restaurant, by throwing another question or topic at Clarice.

They had been walking along the bank now for about fifteen minutes, the footbridge that would take them back to the high street, and to Junji's car, was only a little further ahead. Clarice was disappointed Junji hadn't made his move yet, and she was even more disappointed he had chosen now to bring up her mother.

She shrugged and answered. "I don't know. It's been a while."

"How old were you when the …" he trailed off, then came back with, "when whatever happened, happened?"

From the way he had calculatingly stumbled over his words while asking his question, Clarice could tell what Junji really wanted to know.

So far, the only thing Clarice had divulged about her mother was that she was a trauma amputee, and she had begrudged divulging that much, but on their first date Junji had asked if she lived alone and the surprise on his face when she told him she lived with her mother made her feel compelled to explain why.

Now, plainly, he wanted to know the gory details of how her mother's limb was lost. But instead of coming right out and asking Clarice, he had craftily made a show of his ignorance about the matter, hoping she'd voluntarily enlighten him. *Shrewd!*

"I think I was about eighteen when it happened," Clarice answered, without further explanation.

The awkward silence, relieved only by the sound of the running canal, returned.

"Did I mention how beautiful you look tonight," Junji said after a while.

"You did," Clarice answered.

Junji stopped walking. Clarice did too. He turned to face her.

"I meant it," he said, staring into her eyes, "you look ravishing."

His head began to make an approach toward hers.

Finally, he was making his move, but it was too late, Clarice's willingness to be seduced was gone, her receptive mood had passed, partly because the topic of her mother had been raised, but mostly because of what she was now seeing out of the corner of her eye.

"Stop," she said.

Junji backed away. "Sorry—"

"No, its fine," Clarice said quickly, "I want you to, but," she motioned her head up the towpath, toward the bridge, "I think they're watching us."

Junji looked up the towpath and saw two grungy figures standing on the bridge, staring down at him and Clarice from behind the parapet.

"Maybe we should go back," Clarice suggested, not liking the look of the two figures, "let's leave the way we came in."

"Why, because of them?" Junji asked, his voice becoming robust with male bravado. "They're kids; they're nothing to worry about."

He clutched onto her left hand with his right, and then, almost dragging Clarice along with him, began to march toward the steps which led up to the bridge.

"Halt," said one of the bridge dwellers as Junji and Clarice neared the top of the steps, "this is a vampire checkpoint. You must prove your humanity before you can go any further."

Junji laughed, and though she didn't join him, Clarice could see why. Fresh-faced and probably barely out of school, their two accosters were exactly what Junji had called them; kids.

Long haired and wearing a Slayer t-shirt under his olive-green army surplus shirt, the one who had spoken was wielding a large silver crucifix, which looked like something he had swiped from a church. The armaments of his shorter haired companion, however, a wooden stake and mallet, looked like they were taken right out of a vampire movie.

"What nonsense!" Junji said. "Who's given you this authority; to waylay people like this and make demands of them?"

"The AFDL," answered the shorter haired youth carrying the stake and mallet. "We are members of the Anti-Vampire Defense League."

"The Anti-Vampire Defense League," Junji said, with a tone full of mockery, "when did that start?"

"We had our inaugural gathering tonight," said the crucifix carrier, "we were founded to keep this town free of bloodsuckers."

Junji roared with laughter.

"Fine," he said, "I'll play along." He reached out and grabbed the crucifix. "There, have I proved my humanity now?"

The kid in the Slayer t-shirt nodded. "You may pass," he said, before turning to Clarice. "Your turn."

He held the crucifix out to her.

"Wait," Clarice said, pulling her own crucifix out from her blouse, "I've got my own cross, see?"

She squeezed the pendant into her palm and held it there tight, though this gesture didn't seem to impress the young vampire hunter much.

"That crucifix doesn't means shit," he said, "that's gold. It is silver not crosses that bloodsuckers hate. Haven't you been watching the news? You're going to have to touch this," he jiggled the silver crucifix, "if you're going to convince us, hot stuff!"

Clarice let go of the necklace. The pendant fell against her breast as she sighed.

What else could she do?

She reached out, but instead of taking hold of the silver crucifix, her hand shot passed it, clamped onto the forearm of the obnoxious youth holding the holy item and, with a quick flick of her wrist, broke both his ulna and radius, causing both bones to break the skin.

In unison with his silver crucifix rattling against the moonlit ground, the would-be vampire hunter howled in agony. His cries, though, were quickly silenced as Clarice, like a jungle animal, latched her jaws onto his throat and proceeded to bite through his jugular and carotid artery. Blood poured down his front.

Then, just as she was about to let the now lifeless body in her arms slip through her fingers and become a sprawling, bloody heap on the ground, Clarice felt a pain in her midriff.

She looked down to see a grubby hand holding the handle of a switchblade, the blade of which was buried into her up to the cross-guard.

The shorter haired vampire hunter, the sidekick to one that was now dead, wasn't as gormless as his mouth-breather expression and Limp Bizkit t-shirt suggested. Instead of fleeing, as Clarice had expected him to, he had ditched his ridiculous stake and mallet, wisely recognizing that they would have been useless against her preternatural reflexes, and pulled a switchblade from somewhere, a silver switchblade, judging from the way her wound was smoldering.

Though he was smarter than she had suspected, he still was no Mensa candidate, for he seemed stunned by his own success, and instead of retreating to a safe distance, to assess what damage he had done and perhaps strike again if his prey was appropriately wounded, he merely stood in front of Clarice, eyes wide and mouth agape, seemingly waiting for her to grab onto his head and twist it until his neck broke with a loud snap, which is exactly what she did.

When she let go of him, he flopped to the ground, leaving his switchblade embedded in Clarice's abdomen.

Clarice had taken his life, but he did not go gentle into that good night and had given her a suitably vicious parting shot.

The knife wound was bad. The silver blade felt like it was setting her innards aflame.

Clarice wrapped her fingers around the switchblade protruding from her gut. The silver rivets in the handle burned her as she touched them, causing her nostrils to flare at the scent of singed flesh. Quickly, she pulled the bloody knife from her abdomen and then immediately let it go, allowing it to clang loudly as it hit the pavement. She then clutched at her side, to try to staunch the flow of blood.

"Clarice?"

The voice was Junji.

She had almost forgotten about him. Almost.

She turned to look at him, hoping that she would not see anything in his eyes that might compel her to leave yet another body on the ground.

"You're a ..." Junji stammered, gasping at her.

She nodded and then staggered as she tried to take a step closer to him.

"I'm—"

Before she could finish what she was about to say, she stumbled and fell.

The moment she hit the ground, Junji came running to her side. He scooped her up into his arms and began to carry her away from the carnage of the two dead bodies.

"Don't worry; you're going to be okay. I'm going to get you some help," he said.

It was the last thing Clarice heard before losing consciousness.

Whereever she was, it was someplace cold and recently sterilized, a chill in the air had turned her skin to gooseflesh, and it reeked of antiseptic.

Junji hadn't been stupid enough to take me to a hospital, had he?

Wearily, her eyelids feeling heavy, Clarice opened her eyes and regretted it instantly. Light flooded into her retinas as if acid were being poured onto them, compelling her to quickly bring her eyelids down again. She then tried to raise a hand to act as a parasol over her eyes before she tried opening them again, but to her dismay, she found she could not move, her wrists and ankles were manacled.

To discover where she was, why her limbs had been restrained, was an imperative now, and ready to suffer through the agony of the bright light on her photophobic retinas, Clarice opened her eyes.

Though she squinted, the light still smarted, but she stubbornly endured the discomfort in order for the blurry shapes in her vision to become clear.

When that finally happened, Clarice was able to confirm what she had begun to suspect; she was naked and lying supine on an operating table in a surgical theatre, a makeshift surgical theatre, with two surgical lamps beaming down on her.

"Ah, Miss Daniels," said a confident voice with a clear, well-educated tone, "I see you're awake."

Though she couldn't yet see the body belonging to the urbane male voice, Clarice could sense a presence near her feet.

She craned her neck to look down her body and discovered a lean, elderly man wearing a blue surgical gown standing at the far end of the operating table.

The stranger met her gaze with a confident smile. In his hands, which were wearing surgical gloves, he held a vaginal speculum, a tool of a gynecologist, but the mahogany bookcase full of leather-bound medical texts and the damask wallpaper behind the man screamed to Clarice that she was not in a recognized medical facility, though, even if she had been, her insides would have still been squirming.

This was a home library, she realized, reemployed superficially as a surgery by virtue of having the bare necessities of one, an operating table, surgical lights and a medical tray.

Why had Junji taken me here, to this man?

A few ideas came to her, all of them made her want to cry.

Junji, you bastard!

Tears, though, wouldn't be allowed to flow, not now; now wasn't the time to show weakness.

"May I ask why you have strapped me down to this table?"

As she spoke to her captor, Clarice kept her voice composed and measured.

"Of course, you may," the man with the silver hair and vulpine looks answered. "You've agreed to donate your body to science, to the advancement of human understanding."

"I don't remember doing that," Clarice said.

"Well, you're a little confused at the moment, painkillers will do that; you suffered a nasty stab wound, which I patched up for you."

"Thank you," Clarice said, "but I think I'd like to leave now."

The doctor smiled, and looking at him, Clarice recognized at once that she would not be talking her way out of this loathsome situation. To this man, she was nothing more than a frog for dissecting.

"You don't really want to leave," he said. "We're about to have our names written into history; you're about to become the first female vampire to ever be medically examined. Sure, Oxford has published its findings on that male specimen they have, but every biologist knows, that if you want to really find out the juicy stuff about a species, you've got to get under the skin of the female."

"Help!" Clarice yelled.

Keeping calm had gotten her nowhere, so it was time to try the alternative. Maybe someone in the house would hear her, a wife, a daughter, a son, and have enough compassion to help her.

"Help me, please!" she cried out again but was then silenced by a strip of duct tape, which the doctor placed over her mouth.

"Well," said the doctor, "that was an unfortunate way to end our little chat, never mind." He walked back to the far end of the operating table and again picked up the speculum from off the medical tray. "Well now, shall we begin?" He patted her right thigh familiarly. "I apologize for not having a proper obstetrics chair, this has been all very rushed, but I think we'll manage, don't you?"

A doorbell chimed.

"Who the bloody hell is that, calling at this hour?"

The bell chimed again.

"If that's your boyfriend wanting more money, he can go take a flying leap, I'll tell you that."

Riled, the doctor put down the steel instrument he had just been about to insert into Clarice, snapped off his rubber gloves and marched out of the room, leaving his involuntary patient alone.

Whoever was ringing the doorbell, Clarice was now determined to make their innocuous act a lifesaving one, by turning the temporary reprieve it had given her into a permanent one.

The moment she could no longer hear the doctor's footfalls plodding along the hallway beyond the door, Clarice began to struggle against her thick leather manacles. Her strength, though, usually formidable, was not up to the task of freeing her, not yet. She needed more time to recuperate, without it, the only thing her struggling achieved was to start her stomach wound bleeding again.

It was now that the inevitable thought occurred to her; *I should have stayed in like Mum wanted.* To accompany this admission, she managed a sardonic titter.

Her mother may have been a miserable recluse, but not without a good excuse. She had learned long ago humans were not to be trusted. Indeed, she had learned this in much the same way Clarice was learning it now. Except, when her mother had fallen asleep in her lover's arms, only to wake up and find herself in a sky-lit dungeon, at the cusp of dawn, her left ankle chained to a cast iron stanchion, she had been able to chew her own leg off and escape.

For Clarice, though, escape was beginning to seem beyond her capability.

Goddamn humans! Mum warned me.

But she hadn't listened; she had liked being around them too much. She enjoyed their zeal for life. Most vampires were jaded creatures, but humans, for them, life was but a brief ripple in an ocean, every second was precious.

The sound of footsteps returned to the hallway, only now they were coming toward her, not walking away.

With renewed urgency, knowing this would be her last effort, Clarice again began to struggle against her restraints, hoping to somehow, now things were at their most desperate, find the strength to break free of them.

The door to the room creaked open.

On hearing this, the sound of her hopes being dashed, Clarice's muscles went limp. She knew it was over now.

Wilted and still, eyes closed, stopping the flow of tears, she waited for the examination to begin, for the cold steel of the speculum to violate her, for the beginning of the end.

"I told you it was a bad idea to go out tonight."

Clarice opened her eyes, gasping the word, "Mum."

She then raised her head to gaze upon the figure standing at the end of the operating table.

At first, she thought her mind was duping her, but as she blinked the tears that were clouding her vision out of her eyes, Clarice realized that it really was her mother, not the doctor, who had entered the room.

Blood, lots of it, was dripping from her mouth. But the sight of the gore on her mother's lips didn't alarm Clarice. On the contrary, it caused relief, fresh and invigorating, to wash over her like ocean spray, for it meant the doctor was no longer a concern.

Mother had dealt with him!

The only problem she had to face now was listening to her mother trumpeting, 'I told you so,' at her for the next few days.

Well, it could have been worse, a lot worse.

Ready to take the mater's chiding, Clarice waited for her mother to peel the duct tape from off her mouth and begin the process of unfettering her. However, instead of doing this, the woman with the unkempt hair, bloodstained mouth, and antalgic gait, meandered over to the medical tray where the doctor's various surgical implements were arrayed.

"I tried warning you," she said, picking up a hypodermic needle and a vial of lidocaine from off the medical tray, "but you never listen. You just want to bury your head in the sand and go out and play the sexy vamp. I used to be that way too, remember? I used to have such fun." She was staring off into space as if she could see those fun memories from her past being played out in the distance. "But then I learned the hard way that it's not a safe place out there for our kind. And now that the whole world knows about us, it's going to be a lot worse."

With the hypodermic now primed with lidocaine, Clarice's mother approached the operating table.

"I could have lost you tonight because of your stubbornness," she said as the syringe infiltrated the tissue just above Clarice's left knee. "Perhaps you need what I have; a permanent reminder of the dangers that threaten us, so in the future, you won't be so thoughtless."

Clarice began to squirm, but her squirming couldn't prevent her mother from slowly injecting the anesthetic into her.

After the first infiltration, Clarice's mother made three more before returning to the medical tray, depositing the syringe and picking up a surgical-saw.

"Believe me, child," she said, as she placed the saw's serrated blade against the anaesthetized skin just above Clarice's left knee, "I'm doing this for your own good."

How to Divorce a Dragon

Katie Krantz

Gregory woke up to the smell of eggs cooked by a dragon, an unpleasant yet delicious aroma. Despite his protests, Brenda consistently used her fiery breath to cook the eggs instead of their perfectly good, and rather expensive, stove. Every day, it was the same conversation with the scaly beast.

"You're ruining the sealant," he would say.

"Not badly," Brenda would argue. "The eggs are better this way, and you know it."

"I bought you a perfectly good stove, and you're driving our cooling bill through the roof," Greg always countered. At the beginning of their marriage, Brenda's quirky cooking method was endearing. And the eggs were, to Greg's irritation, delicious.

As he dragged himself out of bed, Greg had to admit that the problem may not necessarily be the eggs or the singed countertop. Perhaps the root of the issue, which he had been ignoring poorly for five years or so, was that Brenda was unmistakably, irrevocably, a dragon. A bright green, scaly, fire-breathing dragon. Greg always thought that their differences would work themselves out, but seven years later, here he was, nauseous at the smell of eggs. Greg could still smell the eggs as he shaved and readied himself for the day. He winced when he hit a patch of burned skin on his ear with the comb.

Getting ready was like trying to swallow the eggs whole in one destructive gulp. His stomach knotted and churned, trying to digest the shell. He prodded his unsmooth skin, trying to will it back into youth with a massage. Greg wished that one day, just one, his wife would give up on making eggs and try something new and exciting, like French toast. In that case, he may not even mind the singed countertop.

Once he was finally passably groomed, Greg headed back to the bedroom. Resisting every impulse to crawl back under the covers, he slipped on his work clothes. His suit pooled around his armpits and waist, tweed scratching against his skin. When he moved to leave the room, he paused for a moment with his hand on the door. He took a deep breath, sweating slightly into his clean dress shirt, and prepared himself to face the dragon.

Brenda was casually standing on her hind legs and blowing fire onto the pan to cook the eggs when Greg pounded down the stairs. When she heard him walk in, the stream of fire stretching from her turquoise lips sputtered to a stop. She smiled at him, innocently flicking her spiked tail to act cute and pretend that she had never once melted a kitchen faucet.

"Good morning, Darling. How are you feeling today? I made you breakfast so that you know I love you." Brenda's tail kept flicking as she sat back onto the floor, her jewel-encrusted belly flashing in the morning light. She squeezed the metal handle of the egg-frying pan unconsciously but hard enough to leave dents that showed when she readjusted her claws.

"Yeah, it's fine," he responded. She breathed out, happy not to suffer through their daily dance of reprimand and defense. Brenda placed the eggs on the stove as though they had been there all along.

"Sunnyside up today!" she hummed, dumping the eggs unceremoniously onto a plate. Greg grunted and slid onto his stool across the counter from her, the only one left unscratched by her and her reptilian friends. He kept his eyes down, working himself up into a frustrated lather about countertop sealant. She sat next to him, and they ate in silence. Greg ate quietly while shoveling the food down, eyes following patterns in the marble as he ignored the metal fork.

"I've already apologized, like, ten times," she said, smoke streaming from her nostrils. She rolled her golden eyes hard enough for them to nearly pop out of her be-scaled head. She snorted, filling the kitchen with even more smoke, tendrils that combined with the wisps coming off of the counter. "It's just a countertop."

On that note, Greg cleaned up his plate and headed out the door.

When Greg fell in love with Brenda in his sophomore year of college, his friends didn't express disapproval so much as disbelief and concern. His fraternity brothers laughed at the preposterous idea that a dragon, or any of the fantastical species' students, would be interested in simple, boring, math major like Greg. When they saw how serious he was about her, even before she knew of his existence, the entire room seemed unnaturally still, even as they pumped the squeaky lever on the keg. Then they burst out laughing at once.

"You got us," they said as they caught their breath. "We thought for a second there that you were serious."

"I am serious," Greg responded, face long. They eyed him suspiciously, hoping he would break out in a grin and assure them he was joking. "She's in my Calc III period, and I'm going to ask her out tomorrow."

"I mean, if that's what you want to go for, man, we'll support you," one responded. They all nodded along in agreement, heads bobbing with their red solo cups, as they quietly came to the consensus that Brenda would never want him back. More than just a dragon, it was rumored that she had done some modeling work with jewelry companies in the past. She was way out of his league. Ran with a different crowd. It would never work out. And anyway, humans and dragons just don't mix well … like that.

For all of his many faults as a husband, Greg always left the kitchen clean before going to work. There was minimal soot on the counter, and he had never allowed Brenda to clean up after cooking his food, even during their worst fights.

Alone in his car, Greg was a different man. He took a moment to clutch his steering wheel with white knuckles. Peeling off the oversized tweed jacket, he reached for his GPS. He plugged in an address that he had found online. Before hitting "GO," he took a moment to de-stress from the morning's interaction.

With every cell in his body, Greg screamed at the windshield of his empty car. It was the kind of scream that a child lets out in frustration after a punishment that is too harsh, because even four-year-olds can show surprising wisdom. He screamed out all of his frustration over scratched chairs and burnt counters and Brenda never caring enough to listen to his one request. It was the kind of scream that starts at your toenails and lets your soul leave your body to take a walk for its duration.

When Greg finished his mini-tantrum, he rested his forehead against the wheel of his Kia and breathed, drinking his soul back into his body. He pulled calmly onto the highway, not letting any more anger slip out. Even when a car pulled out in front of him and proceeded to go twenty miles under the speed limit, he did not let his underlying road rage slip out.

Calmly, carefully, he drove the exact opposite direction of his office and all the way to the Mendelson and Mendelson Divorce Law office.

Before even considering filing for a divorce, Greg had deliberated the move with his drinking buddies. On one Sunday, he gathered them around a TV playing football and distributed beers like military gear to GIs. Brenda was out that afternoon, at one benefit brunch or another, considering where to donate her shed precious jewel scales for charity.

Once the totally unbiased and utterly caring panel had been gathered, Greg muted the commercials to bring up his dilemma. Things just weren't working. He told them everything, from problems in bed (often involving smoke-filled snoring and accidental fireballs) to the all-important egg conflict. He spilled his itemized list of complaints into their beers like a waterfall, but lifted the end of each with a positive statement starting with "but."

"We kind of guessed it wouldn't work out, Greg," said the fraternity brother who had previously defended Greg's affections around the keg. Even though he now drank his beers from cans, he still managed to sip the Kool-Aid as an obnoxious chaser.

"We told you," said his newer drinking buddy, "that spending all night snuggled up against those scales was going to feel wrong. She'll make you feel too soft and week."

"What happens if she accidentally breaths fire while she's, ya know …" Greg's high school best friend made a motion with his hand that would look like a mime of drinking from a can, but with his mouth open wide. "Is that what happened?"

The idea of divorce suddenly became all the more appealing.

Mendelson and Mendelson Divorce Attorneys specialize in interspecies law. Dragon v. human, mermaid v. phoenix, cat v. sphynx, you name it, they sue it. Their offices are located, as one would expect of a skeevy, off-brand lawyer, in a strip mall two exits down the highway from the strip joint capital of the world.

When Greg spotted the firm, the second "e" of the second "Mendelson" had dropped off, leaving only a faded outline of grime. His Kia pulled smoothly into a parking spot directly in front of the cloudy Plexiglas door. Greg tasted copper nerves on his tongue as he walked inside. He crossed the threshold with a fatal blast of an air conditioner to the forehead.

The front room of Mendelson and Mendelson Divorce Attorneys is, in every conceivable way, utterly ordinary. Generic carpeting, neutrally colored chairs with plastic armrests, sun-faded fake plants in the corners. Something about the unoriginal nature of the waiting room layout calmed Greg's nerves. It was like he was wrapped up in a nice big blanket of boring, an assurance of a clear-cut tomorrow that smelled like Lysol spray and stale beer instead of sunny side up eggs and burnt countertop. A little seed of youthful hope grew in his cardiac muscle when he walked up to the counter and signed his name.

"Do you have an appointment?" asked a gruff voice. Greg peered over the countertop to see a stone troll indelicately shove her glasses further up her nose. The plastic bridge ground against her limestone nose, making a grating noise. Her entire face was a collection of pebbles cobbled together by magic, shifting and interlocking to create movement and speech.

"Yes," responded Greg. "It should be under Samson." She punched a few letters into her keyboard, careful not to slam her stone fingers against the computer hard enough to crush the machinery.

"Found it. Sit and wait to be called," she said, gesturing ambiguously into the waiting room. Greg wandered over to a row of chairs, sat, and stared pensively at a drooping, fake fern. He tapped his fingers against the arm of his chair, unsure what to feel. Did it make him a terrible person to be excited? Or did his sadness mean he was making a mistake? Greg's thoughts were interrupted by a crying Gorgon in Chanel sunglasses bursting out of the office room. She was followed by a cloaked, faceless figure that stared at the floor, their hands shoved deep into the pockets of their robes. The door swung closed behind them, and they didn't even look at Greg as they blew out the door.

It only took ten minutes for his name to be called, but it felt more like a decade. The man who called his name was short, balding, and unquestionably human. His warts and large nose and protruding ears were somehow comforting to Greg, who preferred to confide in members of his own species, anyway.

"I'm Mandelson, the elder, and I'm here to help you in any way I can," the little man said, holding the door and motioning Greg into his office. "How can I provide you with my services?"

"Well, um, I'm looking for a divorce."

"Aren't we all?" The lawyer leaned forward on his desk.

"Sure."

"So, can you tell me a bit about your situation? Got charmed by a pixie? I've seen cases where they get nasty once you get to know them."

"Well, actually, it's just not working out anymore. She was my college sweetheart, and, uh, I think it's over." Greg had never said these words outside of the drinking buddy gathering and was surprised how uncomfortable he felt discussing his marital qualms with a near stranger.

"Ah, I see. And what species are we dealing with here? Siren? Succubus? Centaur?"

"Dragon." Mendelson looked shocked. He ran his tiny hands through his thinning hair and sat back in his chair, making it spin from side to side.

"Dragon? Oh boy, we're going to have to be careful about this one." He made some notes on his open legal pad.

"Why is that?" Greg was suspicious of his reaction. Brenda had never done anything dangerous, intentionally at least.

"They can get a bit feisty when cornered. You're absolutely sure you want to go through with this? Have you discussed it with her?"

"Not yet," said Greg, wondering what horrors Mendelson had seen.

"Okay, so before I sign on to take your case, I want you to head back home and work through it with her. I don't want to be anywhere nearby when you serve that dragon divorce papers. Get outta here," Mendelson said, gesturing at the door. Greg walked back to his Kia in a confused daze. *What could the slimy little lawyer have to fear? Getting his warts singed off? That may be a medical favor, honestly.*

When Greg sat in his car, he faced a decision. He had already called in sick to work, leaving himself with two options; driving to a random coffee shop and working remotely until four, or going home to face Brenda. While the former was a fluffy Maltese puppy in comparison to the hike through Hell that represented the latter, Greg's moral compass suddenly activated, compelling him to head back to tell her his thoughts face-to-face.

The drive home was perhaps one of the most painful journeys of his life. Every time he pressed the gas pedal, a tiny voice inside of his head screamed not to and gnawed on his guts in protest.

Back at the house, Brenda's car was still in the driveway. It sat there forebodingly, unmoved since last night. Greg's entire body rejected his opening the door and walking into the house like a stomach squeezing out expired meat.

"Brenda?" he called out into the open house. He could hear her thumping around upstairs and the telltale clink of her claws as she made her way down to the living room.

"Honey, why are you home?" she asked, clearly concerned. Greg generally put in a great effort never to be home early, which had resulted in two promotions and a referral to a marriage counselor by his manager.

"Um, we need to have a talk," he started, guiding her towards the couch to sit. She looked suspicious of his motives. He settled down into the chair across from her, and leaned forward, putting his elbows on his knees. "I think we need a divorce."

Smoke began to stream out of Brenda's nostrils. Greg began to shake. Brenda's eyes flashed an aggressive copper. Greg nearly peed himself. Then, she laughed. Tiny flames wrapped around her sharp teeth. How had Greg never noticed how sharp her teeth are before?

"You're kidding, right? You divorcing me? I can't believe I thought you were serious for a second. That's a good one," she giggled, tossing her head back and blowing more smoke into the air.

"No, I'm serious. I think that things just aren't working out," he said, trying to defend his point. "You just keep burning the counter and not listening to what I need, and I just don't want to do this anymore."

Her laugh stopped.

"You're serious?" she said, a question he knew was rhetorical by the way the tip of her tail was beginning to catch a flame. "You're kidding me. I mean, I knew things weren't perfect, but are you serious right now?"

Greg did not respond. He just watched with horror as the little candle-flame at the end of her tail began to spread up her spines, heating up her gold and gemstone scales. Her sharp talons gripped the couch cushion, and stuffing began to leak out from beneath her claws.

Slowly enough to create a show, she set herself on fire. She stared at the ground, smoke now pouring out of her nose at an alarming rate, setting off the smoke detector on their ceiling. Scale by scale, the flames spread around her body and turned blue. Not knowing what to do, Greg tried to reach out and pat her shoulder but nearly got burned.

The fire eventually started to spread from her body onto the couch. Greg could see why Mendelson had some concerns about divorcing dragons. Looking back, he should probably have thought this setting through a little better. Maybe next to a lake, wearing a welder's mask would have been a little safer. As his carpet, then his window fixtures, then his walls caught fire, Greg could do nothing but observe quietly. This was exactly the kind of thing that made him want to leave Brenda in the first place.

"Could you please stop that?" he asked, folding his arms in front of his chest, moving a foot to avoid the flames slowly spreading to his side of the room.

"How could I, when you broke my heart?" she bellowed, letting more smoke out of her mouth. The gemstones pressed into her chest glinted again, red in the fires. Her flippant response set something off in Greg. If he could have set his chair on fire, he would have. The frustration that brought him to scream in the car flooded back into his soul in full force.

"You're always so self-centered. I've never gotten what I needed from this relationship because I was just too wrapped up in you to care. You know what? I'm DONE with this drama," Greg said, standing up. He stomped out a tiny flame on the carpet next to his foot. "And you know what? When the insurance kicks in to fix this place, which I'm keeping, by the way, because that was in the prenup, I will be cooking all of my food on the stove. And I'll be making something other than eggs. Every. Single. Morning."

Brenda looked shocked. She just stared at him, still sitting on the quickly burning couch, still on fire herself. Greg silently turned around and walked right out the front door. He got back into his Kia and went right down the highway.

He returned to the law office, strode right through the door, and burst into the office. The stone troll tried to call out to stop him but couldn't move fast enough to keep him from his target. Sitting in the chair was some kind of anthropomorphic fox, but Greg didn't care. He stared down Mendelson, whose mouth was open in shock.

"I told her. What's next?" he asked, putting his hands on his hips.

"You should probably call the fire department."

The ki-bad-rá

Kathleen Halecki

The lights flashed on and blinked to announce the news reflecting against the wall and lighting up the room. The announcer's face on the widescreen turned somber, her eyes widening in shock and her full lips, coated with the newest color of the season, pursed together as if she felt hesitant to read from the teleprompter in front of her. Behind her, an image of sharp fangs was projected as the banner displayed in wide black letters, "Vampires Are Not a Myth." After a moment of silence and a deep breath, she continued, "Thank you for joining us on this Friday, May 23, 2025. In our top story, scholars have revealed that vampires are indeed real and not a myth."

She shook her head and attempted to smile, her highlighted hair cascading across her shoulders as she tried to appear confident.

"We will have more details with full coverage on this story coming up within the next hour. Please stay with us."

Lifting his eyes to the screen, Nin did not bother to scan the other stations for additional news. Crossing his long legs, he settled back into the antique leather chair as the screen pulsated with commercials to fill in the time. *Vampires,* he smiled slightly at the thought, his chiseled face, like the marble of Michelangelo's greatest works, drew taut revealing the strength of his jawline as it moved. In the modern era, the word 'vampires' sounded kind, almost matter-of-fact, as if they were a natural part of life and nothing to be feared. No matter where you traveled in the world there was a name for them. There were, in fact, many names in many different languages. In the Eastern lands, the legendary ancestral home of the vampire, it was the Turkish "uber," the Serbian "vuklodlak," the Greek "vroukolkas," the Polish "wieszcry," the Russian "oboroten," and the Romanian "strigoi," to name a few.

The Slavic tribes, terrified by what they saw in the night which could not be explained, believed the crossroads the only safe place against evil, burying those who took their own life there to ensure they would not rise again.

Other tales told within the village warned that you could be born a vampire should you be unlucky enough to come into the world during a certain period of the year or having a cat jump over your body at death.

Still others thought if you ate the sheep killed by a werewolf you would turn, or that you could curse yourself into vampire-hood with your ill-gotten ways, or dying excommunicated from their church. Hundreds of years ago they were referred to as the "Children of Judas," a punishment leveled against his progeny for the betrayal of Christ with a kiss in exchange for thirty marks of silver. Many were destroyed for merely having the crime of red hair. A sure sign of the Devil, for Judas was alleged to have red hair.

Nin could say with certainty that Judas did not possess red hair.

The word vampire was all so … simplistic, but it was not the oldest name for them nor was the drinking of human blood a part of the original story. But the story of their origin and their true purpose, that was a story which had never been told and was a story humans could not yet fathom.

Their most ancient name was long forgotten in the myths and folklore of civilizations. Secrets were never meant to be kept forever, and it now seemed inevitable that after millennia it was to unravel. Once simple stories concocted from the farthest reaches of the human mind were to be swept out into the open. Over the centuries he watched from the sidelines, ever in the shadows of civilization as the legend grew, fueled by events humans could not understand, and the imaginations of storytellers who hoped to allay their own fears that his kind would come for them in the dreaded darkness once the sunset. Their stories brought a romanticism to his unknown world giving characteristics to vampires that they simply did not possess. There was the philosophical, the vengeful, the troubled, the repentant, the soul-sucking, the blood-seeking, and perhaps the worst, the sparkling love-torn eternal teenager.

Their history was buried somewhere in-between the layers woven into the tales. If truth really were to be told, immortality amongst mortals was madness. To watch the hands of a clock with the knowledge that time as it was kept by humans who lived their lives by it meant nothing to you. To stand aside as mortals made the same journey over and over again filled with the same mistakes. Humans were endowed by their creators with the same abilities they themselves possessed, to love deeply and passionately; but their vengeance was something terrible to behold.

His memory was long yet even he could not recall how many times he dispatched those who were left to die by the hands of someone they considered a friend or loved one. They would beg him for mercy to release them from their pain, for which he was more than happy to oblige. He was there from the first war to the late last Great War, watching and waiting to finish the warriors and send them on their way. The blood of so many spilled across the ground as far as the eye could see. Even as he closed his eyes he could imagine the scenes and smell the blood; the taste of iron and rust in his mouth. He drew in a deep breath and licked his lips for the memories filled him with longing.

If the secret was to finally come to light, meant that consequences were to occur for the great goddess had never before revealed her secrets or lifted the veil to humanity. This news indicated that the first sign was upon them and what was to be unleashed upon the world was something unimagined.

He was distracted from his own musings as from within the high rise he could hear his neighbors' exclamations of shock denouncing the news as a hoax, a joke, madness, or some political takeover. They called out to their devices with shrill voices for any information on the current news. Sliders to balconies were slammed shut, and he could make out the faint "click" of the locks to doors and windows as they tried to bar the entrances against any potential threat.

Rising from the chair, he walked across the concrete floors to stare at the numbers gathering below, glued to the lights illuminating from their phones and speaking in high pitches to each other against the heavy traffic of Central Park West. Their hands moved quickly over their screens like spiders across glass. He knew enough about humanity to know that there was a hint of panic emanating from their voices.

Too late.

There was nothing that could save them now from that which was to be released. He drew in a deep breath of the night air, the buttons on his dark shirt struggling to stay within the confines of the holes across his broad chest as he raised his arms outwards. His long ebony-colored hair blew across his face from the heat of the city streets as his eyes scanned the entire length of the horizon. He could smell the car exhaust, the potent scent from the vendors, the smallest trace of the flowers from a girl's perfume, and the pheromone of fear as it began to ooze from the pores of the masses gathering on the street.

Nin waited, listening, and then he felt the winds begin to change direction and then speed up, picking up the debris from the streets below to create cyclones of dust.

Yes, there could be no doubt that Enki was racing ahead of the storm demons to change Enlil's mind again, frantically searching for a way to stop what was to happen.

He drew in another deep breath and spoke the sacred name. The name that was not to be repeated. The name both respected and feared, Ereškigal, Lady of the Great Earth. Speaking her name would give her power in this world, for the signs were clear that the gods met once again after their long slumber in the great congress and made a decision in regards to their creation's fate.

Behind him, the fair-haired announcer returned to the screen, her lipstick refreshed and seemingly more composed as she looked straight at the screen.

"Yesterday, archaeologists uncovered a mysterious limestone door with inscriptions dating back before the oldest known writing. From what they have been able to translate, a warning is inscribed upon the doors announcing that it is the gate to that which was called the 'Netherworld' in Sumerian. Additional clay tablets at the site seem to record accounts of attacks by something called gallu; what scholars are saying seems to be equivalent to our modern vampire. We have been assured that the gate is sealed tightly with no apparent fissures."

She moved her seat to allow a full view of the screen. "We will be going live in a few minutes to western Iran for a better view. Dr. Ahmadi, can you hear us?"

The screen flashed to a young man with a full dark beard, his skin tanned from his time in the sun who was clearly excited to speak to the camera. He stood before an enormous limestone arch appearing to have two doors with various images inscribed onto it carved into the side of the mountain. As the camera panned out then came into focus, the audience could see there were two enormous statues of anthropomorphic figures standing on either side of the entrance. With raised daggers in each of their hands, the top portion of the figures were dressed in armor from the waist up, but what supported the body was not legs, but large scorpion tails poised as if ready to sting.

Nin's steps were quick as he moved closer to the large screen and whispered at the sight of the two stone figures.

"Lugal-irra. Meslamta-ea. How long have you stood there waiting to tear out the heart and compress the kidneys as commanded by Nergal? Your time is soon coming."

The archaeologist nodded as he held his finger over the headphones to listen to the blond announcer.

"Yes, yes, I am here. We are at the base of the Zagros Mountains at a place called Bisotun. This is a UNESCO World Heritage Center and a very important location for thousands of years. The importance is shown by the name which means the 'place of the gods.' An ancient trading route ran for many miles across the area bringing goods back and forth across many empires. We are not too far from the spot where the bas-relief of King Darius I, ruler of the Persian Empire, known as the Behistun Inscription is located. It is just up on the ridge above us and to the right. This relief celebrates his victory over his numerous enemies. It is that 1,200 lines of inscription, and a large number of scholars working on it for many years, which enabled us to be able to translate some of the earliest languages as it was written in Elamite, Babylonian, and Old Persian."

Dr. Ahmadi pointed to the structure behind him.

"Over the last two days, seismic movement in this area has revealed this immense find to us. It is as if the side of the mountain just slipped away from this structure and somehow left the stones completely intact. If you look closely, you can see what appears to be an old road which runs straight into the doors. We have been finding these wonderful cuneiform tablets at the site with many of them documenting what appears to be activities of the gallu. What is curious is that the first mention of the gallu is from the Old Babylonian period when they are described as one of seven spirits in the netherworld. But here we are given information that seems to indicate that they were left on the other side of the netherworld when the gates were shut as some sort of policing agency in order to execute the laws of the great god and to keep watch until the day ..."

Hesitating, Dr. Ahmadi, ran his fingers over one of the symbols on the tablet.

"I cannot quite make out what this says, the word is unfamiliar to me, but it seems there is some sort of day they will be made known to us, or is coming, once the gates open. They also mention the god, Namtar, the destroyer of men through plague, and Pishittu, the demon who eats children at birth, and that these gods aided the gallu to stop us from multiplying too quickly under the command of the god of war, the King of Snakes, son of Ereškigal, Queen of the Great Below."

Dr. Ahmadi lifted his eyes from the tablet to look back into the camera.

"These are really incredible finds and give us great insight into the cosmology of the Sumerian world. The text declares that they speak to those in the future as a warning of what might come. Apparently, they did believe these creatures were real. Of course, we have yet to see anything, but we may have uncovered a massive gravesite here. The Sumerian script alleges this to be the ki-bad-rá[1] or the realm of the dead. What is really fascinating is that we have always thought of the Sumerian netherworld as something quite intangible, although they always associated the dead with the mountains which is kur in Sumerian, with some of the text seeming to depict the place of the dead as a real mountain. Many of the Sumerians described a foreign road as leading to the dead, but the idea of an ancient road to a physical place seemed highly improbable until now. I see no apparent way into the gate. However, we are scanning now to see what is behind the structure."

From the dark recess of Nin's memory, the ancient words he had not spoken in eons began to roll off his tongue. The words that were written on clay tablets, baked in the sun by priests who recorded their deeds.

"ki-ùr kur-ra ke kùkku-zu-ḡen-ba, (Go to your darkness, at the base of the netherworld)."

Although the dead passed easily into the ki-bad-rá, few dared to enter the gates and be returned to the living. Only Inanna, thinking to trick her sister into making her queen in her stead, and for which she was punished, and the mighty king Gilgameš who begged entrance at the door seeking to find his lost friend, Enkidu. The door was the first step on the way to eternal life and only meant for those dead to begin the long journey.

"urugal ig-gal-àm igi-ḡà ba-am-gub ur nu-mu-an-da-'e" (The tomb is a big door; it stands in front of me, it does not let me ascend.)

Staring at the foolish scholars milling about the structure as they scanned for any way inside, he could only think, *you will not like what you will find. dingir-ku-ra lù-ga-gu-me-eš ... the gods of the kur are man-eaters.*

Nin kept his dark eyes on the statues behind the man with bated breath for he knew why they were positioned as sentinels outside the doors. The humans did not understand that it was not for them to open the gate from the outside; the gate was opened from the inside and only by Bitu who waited to pull back the mighty bolts. The movement they felt was the trembling of the first of the doors of the palace ganzir being opened to allow for her, nin-kur-ra, to pass. They did not know that it was the start of the great awakening caused by the noise of humanity who once more plagued Enlil with their endless sins and tumultuous voices.

Humans prided themselves on their high technology while they lost their souls. They had not yet learned to live and seek pleasures in the world for they pushed their mortality out of their minds. They did not seem to understand that in knowing that death was coming for you was how you learned to live each day well. Although they advanced in their tool-making, they were still like children, fighting and grasping at each other for every little scrap that came their way and forgetting their creators.

They shouted and screamed as each tried to make their voice heard above the others forgetting the sacredness of words. The sound was so overwhelming he could barely think over the din of their voices. It came as no surprise that the sound would wake the great gods and enrage Enlil.

He had watched as the natural order of cities were lost to chaos causing them to fall to ruin and decadence, the covenant between ruler and commons broken. He watched as the widows and orphans were left to fend for themselves, forgotten by the wealthy who took advantage of their weakness. There were far less of them when Enlil first set plagues upon the land then withered the grain in the fields after refusing to give rain, and the people grew restless and hungry crying out against the great gods. It was then Enlil decided to destroy them with the great deluge.

It was only through the kindness of Enki, Lord of the Earth, feeling compassion for the creations who rushed to send a dream of warning and whispering the plans to Ziusudra to build a gufa and load up the animals. It was because of this action that these feeble creatures were saved. The story, handed down in various forms, was meant as a warning yet it went unheeded generation after generation although it was often told and familiar to many.

Enlil was softened after seeing the destruction caused by the flood and humans flourished again, but the great gods were temperamental and their minds easily changed.

Nin raised himself to stand to his full height in front of the screen as he felt a sense of being renewed in his purpose. How long he had suffered the noise of these humans as he obeyed the voice of the great gods and fulfilled his duty once the doors closed? Born of Eriškegal, his full name was Ninazu, he only called himself Nin in order to live amongst the earthly creatures, trying to understand and know them better as time passed. Life and death were not meant to walk so closely along the same path and living among humans caused him anguish as he roamed from place to place.

His cult centers were once celebrated at Ur, Enegi, and Ešnunna, and his name glorified by those whom he helped in their wars, but as humans neglected the ways of their ancestors, his name passed from memory. Offerings were once burnt on his altars and worship flourished in his temples until the people stopped believing. As the libations disappeared, with no wine or water provided, his anger grew at those who were so neglectful. When offerings were not given, they needed to be taken.

Many pronounced a curse upon them, even in the early days of humans before the bolt was placed across the seven gates, crying against them in their lamentations.

"gallu šu-ni ma-ra-an-túm-a áš-hul-bi hé-en-dug," (May a vile curse be pronounced upon the gallu who brought this hand against you.)

The gallu did not listen to prayers and accepted no offerings as they had no mercy, being but shadows of darkness. The gallu had no family so taking the lives of loved ones meant nothing to them. The sorcerers only tricked the people who came to them for help for the gallu were created to roam the streets of the living, selecting their victims, and snatching them away, and none of the incantations performed could prevent them from doing so.

His own increasing silence as he fell into despair waiting for events to unfold left the gallu doing his bidding only out of respect for him as their creator.

Even without knowing why they were created they listened when he spoke, and no human rituals could stop what the gods demanded.

Year after year, century after century, he waited patiently not knowing if the day would ever come when the endless drone of those who were created would cause Enlil to demand they be silenced. Although the gallu took as many as they could under cover of darkness, the earth was overrun and the time had finally come for the gates to be opened and the full force of the Anunnaki, the lesser gods dwelling in the ki-bad-rá, be given free rein over the living.

That would not be all that would be coming, for behind them would come the vengeful dead, those whose funerary offerings were neglected and who suffered from the torments in the netherworld.

Why did these humans think their lives were filled with sorrow knowing nothing but ill-health and bad humor? They forgot their ancestors they minute they were laid into the ground and made to fend for themselves.

The priests who knew the sacred words at the temple were no more, and there was no one to recite the prayers to comfort the dead or observe the proper rites. Families divided their inheritance, squabbling over the goods they could not bring with them all the while forgetting that they themselves would soon be etemmu and their bodies nothing but bones. Then they would feel the great hunger and thirst and cry out for offerings only to find that their wailing was met with the same silence.

The dead in the ki-bad-rá were angrier than they had ever been before and soon, they would be able to satiate their thirst.

He pulled his feet out from his boots to stare at his talons. At the beginning of civilization, kings called upon his divine help, but the days of raising up a man to kingship who would honor and heed the words of the gods were long since passed. When he had been called upon to aid his followers, he came as a muš-ḫuš (fierce dragon), and the time had come to show these humans what he could become when he came into battle.

Climbing onto the railing he sat there, perched, overlooking the city. There were few who actually knew what the gallu looked like, although the horrors of their actions were always described, the creations would see his warriors in their full form. If Enlil was merciful and there were any who might live through the night, they would remember and write down what took place during the time of the gallu, led by the King of the Snakes.

Threads began to unravel across his back as if stretched upon a rack and he moved his shoulders until a crunching sound could be heard. The fibers danced away and were picked up with the dust as his enormous dark wings began to expand. From the corner of his eye he could see the blonde announcer again, her glossy lips moving as if ready to speak, then she began to scream as she pointed at the screen. Ninazu could see the statues moving in the background their tails shaking violently back and forth, and the archaeologists recoiled in horror as they noticed the movement dropping their equipment as they attempted to run, tripping over wires and equipment in doing so.

At that moment, Ninazu knew that Enlil could not be moved to spare them despite the protest of Enki. He watched emotionless, feeling not a flicker of pity, as Lugal-irra and Meslamta-ea raised their arms high striking their blades into the closest scholar within their reach whose mouth fell open in shock and disbelief as the stone daggers ripped open his chest to expose his still-beating heart. The camera began to wobble, and Dr. Ahmadi screamed for everyone to move back as the doors began to slowly swing open as if by invisible hands.

Ninazu smiled grimly as he recognized his mother emerging, her long dark hair wrapped in chains of silver and her arms raised upwards as the Anunnaki came from behind her in a mad rush. The visual was cut off, and the city descended into an odd silence as the lights flickered along the street and people looked around in confusion unsure of what had just taken place or what was to come.

In the far distance, Ninazu could hear thousands of wings breaking through the night air which was followed closely by screeching from the slamming of brakes and the crackling of fiberglass. As the sound drew closer, the screams from below rose up as one and then came the agonizing cries of death lifted up on the wind as Enki wept. Rising up, he spread his wings to their full span and took flight to take his fill.

[1] Translations from Dina Katz, The Image of the Netherworld in Sumerian Sources, (New Haven: CDL Press, 2003).

The Red Blizzard Returns

Abiran Raveenthiran

Part One: A Blizzard Forecasted to Never Return

Shia lifted the newspaper in efforts of avoiding conversation with her co-worker, Ted. She had felt a sense of hunger for months now. No matter what she ate, she was left feeling unsatisfied. She ate, but it was never what she felt she was craving. The problem was she didn't know what she was craving. The worst of it was, Ted's insistent chatter only bugged her more.

"Could you believe that Smilodon saved my kid the other day? A stalker woman, Edeena Richarche kidnapped my kid and pow; Smilodon walks right in and takes her back," said Ted. He spoke louder noticing Shia look through the paper. She briefly looked up at the man with an unhealthy hue of skin. She often wondered if the sun had ever so much as touched his skin. Yet, who was she to judge? Her skin was almost as pale. The only difference was, she was putting in the work at spray tans to add some color.

Ted repeated it as if he was telling it the first time. Shia had been surprised and astounded, but the continuous retelling had become annoying.

"Edeena. Kidnap. Saved. Got it," Shia said sounding bored but not meaning to. She looked through the newspaper to find something interesting. Anything would be better than having this conversation again. *Wendigoes and Their Diet—Humans, that was simple enough. Indian Lost Ancient Civilization: The Sun People—could be worth the read maybe I'll come back to that one.*

"Oh, my god. Look at the front page," said Ted. His misshaped head peering over the top of the newspaper. Shia turned it over and read, 'A Blizzard Forecasted Never To Return.'

Ted read over her shoulder as she read.

'Red Blizzard, named after the killing spree of a woman in her mid-20s by the use of manipulating snow and ice, has been missing for months. Many citizens fear that she could be plotting something bigger. In our recent interview with Smilodon, we know it to be different.

We have sources confirming that Red Blizzard was first seen after killing a prominent businessman in cold blood two years ago. Since then, she has targeted many.

Smilodon, our beacon in this blizzard, states, "The situation has been taken care of. Trust me. The citizens of Vancouver can sleep peacefully. Red Blizzard will never be seen—'

The building shook. So subtle that Shia didn't notice. Then, the vibrations got worse and worse.

"What's going on?" Ted asked. He grabbed onto Shia's arm.

"Earthquake!" The building started to crumble. Parts of the drywall and concrete fell to the floor.

"Quick. We have to get out of here."

A portion of the wall fell down. Right onto Ted's leg. His glasses broke as he fell and he whimpered on the floor, like an injured puppy. He may be annoying, but that didn't mean she wanted to see the man die.

"Go on. Leave without me," Ted said. His mouth said one thing, but she saw in his eyes that he didn't truly mean it. That was the thing about people. Their eyes told you what they truly meant.

"No. We are going to get out of here," Shia said, grasping his arm. "The both of us." Shia stopped and stared at the blood leaving his leg. It was red and glistened in the light. The fruity aroma was what pulled her in. It spilled onto the floor, like a bottle of tannic red-wine. Shia could feel her mouth as dry as the Sahara Desert. She licked her lips, but it did little good.

The sound of someone's voice snapped her to attention. Except, it wasn't Ted's. She looked up to see a man, half-human half-large cat—Smilodon. His appearance was that of a human with golden fur with only the head swapped with that of a wild jungle cat. She felt light-headed but knew Smilodon was pulling her and Ted out from the building. His claws dug into her skin, but with the adrenaline of the moment, she barely felt it. That and her hunger. Hunger hit her almost instantly. It fought to come out like a caged animal that hadn't been fed for days; then set its eyes upon its first meal.

Shia looked down at her finger. It was stained red. The world began spinning as she grew even more light-headed. She held on tightly to her hero to steady herself. The hunger didn't return because it was always there. The blood was more of a reminder, and that of one she couldn't ignore. Then, she slowly placed her finger in her mouth.

Everything came back to her, all at once. First, the memory of a different life, one not so human. Memories of not being the prey, but a predator returned. A life of Smilodon killing her family and friends returned. The memory of Smilodon holding her child above his head and then twist her back returned.

The last was a memory of Smilodon mumbling words under his breath and touching her with a ring embedded with a green gemstone. It was a spell of some sort, magic even. For certain, Shia could not tell. What she did know was that Smilodon had wiped her memories clean. He had taken away who she truly was and only left a shell of a person behind. A person who lived a normal life. A person who was imprisoned to live a normal life.

He may have been a savior for the humans, but for the race of Wendigoes, he was their cause of near extinction. Was it their fault that their source of food was humans? It was biology. It was the way of the jungle. No hero had the right to change that.

Shia returned to the present, only to see Smilodon still carrying her. Her eyes made its way to the eerily glowing green ring. It was all the confirmation she needed.

Everything was so easy now. It was all within her grasp.

"Even if you take away everything, a predator will always be a predator," Shia whispered before twisting the so-called hero's neck. *Who had known that it would have been so simple? A twist of the neck and years of fighting and warring was over.* Odd that even after she had gotten her revenge for stealing her memories, the feeling of fulfillment hung in the air.

His body fell to the ground in a slump. She expected something more to occur. A hero, one of the best of his time, had fallen. Except, all that she received was a pair of eyes that stared right back. Empty.

A white light arose from his body. It looked like a large worm wiggling its way out of a tight hole. It writhed back and forth. She knew what to do. It was almost instinct. Shia bent down and slurped his soul through her mouth. Her hunger was satisfied. The gnawing hunger subsided. It hadn't completely disappeared, but now the beast was tame.

A whimper from behind reminded her of another. She looked back and saw a pale Ted shivering as though he saw a monster. Then, she remembered, she was one. She walked up to him and snapped his neck.

Shia, The Red Blizzard, the Wendigo is back, she thought as she looked to see both her 'co-workers' bleed out into the snow.

Part 2: Edeena

Shia had returned. The superhero, Smilodon, had removed her memories altogether; but she had seen to his demise. It was one that had felt to be unfulfilling after so many years of trying to best him.

Now, she yearned to remember who she was. Her memory was returning in fragments. Who was she? The answer had still been left unanswered. Or, answered with only tidbits of information.

She had not been sure how to find the patches of memory that eluded her up until a few days ago. Her thirst for blood had led her into an alleyway with a drug dealer. With each soul that entered her system, she remembered more and more. Each soul fell into place like a puzzle piece. The issue was, she hadn't realized how vast this jigsaw puzzle was.

Compared to the average human, it spanned lifetimes.

The first recollection of memories had occurred with the ingestion of only a drop of blood. This time, was different. She had memories that she remembered, but this was different. This was a little girl by the name of Ember in a far-off land. The little girl shared the same fiery red hair as her but was also different.

The more she discovered, the less sense everything made. Why did she remember memories that did not belong to her?

The answer to that question would only be answered by a third victim. This time also a man who would likely not be looked for immediately. This Edeena Richarche was the same woman who had supposedly kidnapped Ted's daughter. She was a computer hacker who spent most of her days in his room roaming the web under the alias of HotRod69. She also appeared to be doing more than just roaming the web with that name.

Using the alias, she scoured the web for women. Younger women by the looks of it. HotRod69 was a cougar who had a taste for innocent 'kitties.' She spent her days luring beautiful women; catfished to believe Edeena was really Ed—a male. She wouldn't do anything except watch her from afar. Just stare and then leave as though that was enough to feed her fetish.

If anything, Shia was doing the world a service. Who knows what a meaty old woman scouring the web was truly looking for.

She slipped into the room and before HotRod69 even realized it and snapped her neck. There was a series of gurgles until only silence kept Shia company. Her soul wiggled its way out, as it did for Smilodon.

For some reason, that was related to her forgotten powers. There were still more gaps to fill her jigsaw puzzle of memories. She intended to fill the gaps with the blood of her 'big-boned' victim.

She slurped it before and was transported into another set of memories. She sat in the memories like she always did, like a backseat driver of a car. The memory took its course, and Shia observed. There was one thing that was odd though. Extremely, odd. The clothing, the style of everyone around her. It appeared as if she had traveled back fifty years.

She looked at a mirror. Shia looked the same, with the exact same features except somehow more beautiful. Her fiery red hair was done neatly in curls. Her purple dress, which contrasted against her red hair and pale skin, hugged her bust and cut off just above the knees. In one word, she was beautiful and based off of the looks from the men in the room, she wasn't the only one who noticed.

After being pushed by his group of friends, one had summoned up the nerve to come speak to her.

"Hello, sweetie. My name is Rodney. You can call me—"

Shia cut him off instantly. "That's great and all Rodney. If it was any other night, I would've torn your clothes off and rode you like the sports car you clearly don't own. Except, today I am a little busy hun. How about we do this another night? Call me."

Rodney stared at her with his mouth open. He realized as he followed Shia's gaze back to his own mouth and closed it.

"What are you busy doing then?"

Shia made a sideways glance at another man. He had slicked back hair and a jaw that had probably been chiseled by God himself. His skin glistened like diamonds and wore red on black clothing.

"I wish I had the time to explain. Except, I don't."

Rodney smirked a bit. "Try me. There are many things you probably don't know about me."

Shia let a bit of air escape her lips as though it were a laugh. "Really? You think I haven't already figured you out? Based on the people you are hanging around with who urged you into a task they doubt you would have completed successfully, you are probably a guy who works all day behind a computer. You barely come out and don't enjoy it either. The only reason you came out tonight was that the group finally asked you and you took it as an opportunity to make friends. That was even the reason you took the challenge to come talk to me."

"That was amazing. Right again. For the most part," Rodney answered.

The man with diamond skin rose from his table and began walking toward them.

"Leave," Shia said abruptly. She attempted to shove Rodney with one hand discretely, but he never took the hint.

"What makes think I'll leave as soon as you call to me?"

Shia looked deep into his eyes. There was a seriousness in her tone now. She leaned in so no one else would hear what she had to say. "No one knows where it came from, or whether or not it is just a legend. It is said that there's a presence that secretly ruled over households for generations. I've met it, in the dark eyes of a stranger. I'm willing to risk my entire life finding out what it wants of me. I am not ready to risk yours. So. Leave."

He wore a perplexed expression but stood as dumb and idiotic as a rock.

The man with diamond skin had walked up to them. Realization slowly overtook Rodney as he looked into the other man's dark eyes. The eyes of a stranger. The eyes of a legend, *the* legend.

He placed his crimson red drink on the table and leaned into Shia.

"I know what you are. I even know who you are. So, I'll return the favor. My name is Vladious. I have no doubt that you are here to kill me. Or at least try to. I warn you, leave and don't look back."

"I can't. It had taken me too long to track you. Your kind does well in hiding yourselves."

This brought a grin to Vladious's pale face. "As do yours."

They both stared into one another's eyes. There was no love. There was pure hatred. However, in Rodney's there was confusion.

Vladious attacked the men at the nearest table with almost lightning speed. He held the beating heart of one man in his hand. Even the heart hadn't realized it had been separated from the rest as it released a few more pathetic heartbeats in his hand. The surrounding people were taken by shock. Rodney had missed the whole movement in one blink. If he had not overheard their conversation, he would have assumed the splattered blood was spilled crimson alcohol.

Shia had not missed any of it. She was just not prepared to act. If she did, it would have been Rodney's heart in his hands. The pathetic fool had grown on her. This way, she was in control of the fight. She was in more control than he will ever know.

The room was in chaos as a woman's scream confirmed the rest of the people's thoughts. The screaming people fled in all directions.

A grin formed on Shia's face. A grin of self-satisfaction.

"Why are you smiling?" Vladious asked.

"Because Vladious. You just confirmed my thoughts. Now, we can have a good old-fashion fight. Plus, even if you do manage to get away, I doubt you can show your face in these parts again. Your move was too out in the open. Checkmate."

Vladious laughed and slurped on a large vein hanging from the heart as though it were a straw. "Oh, you fool. We are going to kill everyone here."

"We?" Shia asked. As if on cue, a dart came flying across the room. Rodney kicked her chair causing the dart to narrowly pass Shia's head. She fell to the floor.

"You could have just pushed me," she grumbled.

It was a blur of a fight for Rodney. Shia jumped across the room and tore through some of them. She was brilliant. She was fast, even faster than Vladious and his vampire friends. They were fast. But she was faster.

One crept behind Shia. He was close enough to attack. Rodney grabbed a fork and stuck it into his hand. The scream caught Shia's attention. With one swift move, she turned and decapitated the vampire.

Shia held an edge of a table and shoved it into one of their chests. She had swiftly and effectively taken out most of the group by herself with the help of Rodney for one of them.

"Let him go," Vladious growled.

"Or what?"

"I'll suck the blood out of this one's throat," Vlad said, grasping tightly onto Rodney. Shia's eyes met Rodney. Yet, she didn't see fear. There was hope. Hope that she would save him.

"Foolish human," she whispered under her breath. "I will not stop just for one life. There are so much more at stake." She said the words but did not feel that way.

Rodney shivered. He had never experienced this much. His life was the computer then home. "I know we just met and I know we don't even know each other's names but … I think I love you."

Shia decapitated the vampire.

Vladious growled and lunged at Rodney. Shia moved as fast as she could to save Rodney. Her eyes followed the vampire's fangs. It got closer and closer to Rodney's neck. Shia was much too far away to make it in time. Tried she did, but she would never make it. There was just too much distance between them.

Vladious's fangs got closer to Rodney's neck. Except, Vladious miscalculated something. His fangs had assumed something to be there that wasn't. The Adam's apple was missing. That miscalculation was just enough for Vladious's fangs to graze Rodney's neck and miss.

Shia jumped at the vampire. He turned and pushed Rodney at Shia. The force sent him flying. Shia ran to check on Rodney's wellbeing. He lay on a wooden table that had broken under the force.

"Did you get him?" Rodney asked.

She shook his head. "He got away. I'll hunt him later."

She fell to the ground and lay beside Rodney who lay there almost breathing in and out from exhaustion.

After a few seconds, Shia spoke. "What was the one thing I got wrong in my guess about you?" Somehow, she knew the answer. Still, she wanted to hear it from the source.

"You said I was a guy who worked behind of a computer." Rodney paused and smiled. "I am a woman who works behind a computer."

Shia let out a little laugh. Of course, that was the reason. She should have seen it. The curves were hidden, but the features of a woman still remained with full lips, full lashes and no Adam's apple.

"You barely know me. How could you say you love me?"

"Because this experience was the first I never had to fake being something else. As a woman, I have to pretend to be something I'm not in life. The fight. The adrenaline. It's all a different experience. That's thanks to you."

"What's your name? Your real one, I mean."

"Edeena Richarche. I never did get to use my pickup line."

"Go for it," Shia said.

"My name is Rodney. You can call me Rod. Hot Rod. Let's take out the 1900's from this year and 69."

Shia laughed. "That's horrible."

"I know."

Shia got up and limped her way out.

"So, I will never see you again. Will I?"

Shia shook her head. "It's safer that way."

"I will find you. One day or the next. I really do love you."

"No. You won't and don't. Goodbye, Hot Rod."

The memory ended and Shia rose from the body of her meaty victim. Edeena Richarche. The woman who had spent her entire life searching for stupid, old Shia. Too bad Shia had found her first.

She held the woman in her arms. Blood stained her clothes except she didn't care. All she wanted was Edeena back. With one finger, she touched her uvula to induce vomit. Nothing came. There was no way to return the soul of a good woman. A woman who didn't deserve this to happen to her.

Part Three: Vladious

Shia stared at a small house that was just on the outskirts of the city. The rain washed over the dreary setting, causing the trees outside to droop even more. It was a reflection of how she felt inside. She wanted to droop for what she had done. She wanted to succumb to the circumstances that revolved around her. Yet, she stood against it.

She pushed the door open, sending a creek into the night. It was an odd feeling. She had been invited to this house on various occasions but never took it upon herself to actually come. Maybe this whole thing could have been avoided.

The house was dark. None of the lights were powered, and gloomy weather outside only added to the atmosphere. Shia saw an outline of a person.

"You came," the voice said. "You finally came."

Shia walked up to the man. Except, he was no man. His skin glistened like diamonds even in the darkness. "Vladious."

He laughed, practically cackled. "That's a name I haven't heard in a long time. Why don't you call me by the name you use? Ted." Even in the darkness, Shia could see his smile.

"Why?" That was all Shia wanted to know. Why lead her through so much pain and misery? Why not tell her everything from the beginning? Why send her to kill Edeena?"

He laughed again. It only brought anger to Shia. She had to hold herself back from ripping his head off. At least until she got what she wanted from him. He eyed her clenched fist.

"Tell me. Did the fat lady sing when you ripped her apart? I only wish I could have seen her face. Or even your face. It must have been just as good."

Her blood was boiling with fury. She took steps towards Vladious. He had once been a co-worker in a regular life. She should have seen it. If she had dealt with him before, maybe Edeena would still be alive.

She gritted her teeth and repeated her question. "Why?"

Suddenly, he rose from his chair. The force knocked it sideways. "Why?" He shouted. "Why? Could you understand what you did to me that day in the bar? You took everything from me. Everyone I ever knew. Everyone I ever loved. I waited for the day to exact my revenge. Then, I came upon you. You were clueless. I could have snapped your neck right then and there. I almost did. Except, I wasn't sure if that would even kill you. I'm not even completely sure what you are. I could have snapped you out of your trance at any point in time. What would the fun in that be? Even if I did kill you, you would never know what it would be for. So, I tried to snap you from your trance every day. I repeated Edeena's name, seeing if that would trigger anything. Nothing." He walked over to the corner of the room and poured scotch in a glass. He swirled it and took a few sips.

"Then, I tried to feed you bad stories about Edeena. Maybe even get you to kill her. It would be a slow progression. Then, when you broke out of your trance, you would realize you killed her, and you could live the rest of your pathetic immortal life drooling over her. Who knew that Smilodon would be the one to break you out? I never expected you to go on a rampage like that. That was just luck. A whole lot of luck. I thought you would have realized once you saw no soul come from me. Except, in your bloody rage, you didn't care."

He swung back a few more shots. "Well. I'm ready." He stood with his hands apart. "Kill me. Kill me now."

In a blink of his eyes, she was upon him. She could have torn his head off right then and there. Shia's hands held onto his head. Then, she stopped. She released him.

He looked as surprised as she was.

"I'm not going to kill you, Vladious. That would just be too easy. I've killed a lot of people. No. I don't think you deserve the same pain that they endured. You're something worse. Something completely worse."

He spat to the floor. "You think you're better than me? We both feed on humans."

She nodded, "I never said I was a saint. I'm going to give you a punishment. Something far worse."

His eyes widened. There was fear in it. Fear. She relished it.

"I'm going to let you live. Live alone. Live knowing that you are the last of your kind. Live as the last one. I've killed all your disciples. I saw to that before I came here today. I'll make sure you'll never be able to create another vampire. Live and suffer, Vladious. You wanted me to be your way out. I'm not going to give it to you."

Shia then did the hardest thing she had ever done in her life. And that truly meant something considering the length of it. Of course, her memory was still not fully intact. Shia turned and walked away from the vampire. Who fell to the floor, defeated.

Vampires of Sacramento

Leslie D. Soule

"**G**ood evening, everyone. Thank you for tuning in. We have reports coming to us from a handful of nations now, that vampires are in fact, real. That's right, going into this year's Halloween season, it'll be hard to tell if that vampire coming to your door is a costume or the genuine article …"

Immediately, a thousand thoughts raced through my mind. *This can't be real. Vampires? What in the world has our news media become?* I already loathed the traditional, 'dinosaur' media of television, that often delved into sensationalism in order to gain viewers back in a desperate attempt to stay relevant to modern culture. *There was a reason I'd taken citizen journalism courses. What is this garbage?* I shook my head in disgust. But then the program kept right on, like one of those boring programs about the latest horrific events of the city.

"Reports are coming out of central Sacramento, California, and out of New Orleans, Louisiana, out of our neighbors to the north in Canada, out of New Zealand and London, England."

Why did they have to say Sacramento? Why did this vampire scourge have to have originated here? All at once, I became overwhelmed with thoughts of the past, and the time it took me back to, and my breath came out in ragged bursts. There was one person, who could have passed for a vampire, but he'd been relegated to that old memory vault. "No," I said, pushing the thoughts away, trying my best to will away the implications of these vandal considerations. *Thinking about this will do me no good. There was no way he could have survived, could have made it through all these years, could have found his way to an actual vampire and then spread the curse of vampirism, here, to this boring old city that couldn't decide if it wanted to be a country cowtown or San Francisco.*

But eventually, I had to come to grips with reality, and all that it entailed.

"He's come back," I whispered to myself, realizing the dire truth that the news media proclaimed. It meant that a man named Dave Micker had not actually died. Well, that's not entirely true either. *He died, supposedly of brain cancer. I'd read the announcement years ago, on his old MySpace page—that had to have been back in like 2008.* But now it was September of 2025, and MySpace was a thing of yesteryear, as forgotten as 8-track tapes and cassettes.

So, what do I do, now?

I drove down the road and passed the old 'vampire' haven on Mine Shaft Road. A huge building that was once a multi-use space with a mini-golf course attached to it. Now, the tiny buildings on the golf course were falling apart. Some had tree branches running through them. The old fountain ran dry, these days. And I wondered if anyone knew about the dance floor that lay hidden beneath the place, where young men and women used to hang out and role play, playing the Vampire. The masquerade game by White Wolf. A LARP ran on these grounds, and the crowd was in their young 20s, dressed in black and pretending to belong to one of the many vampire sects of the game.

I shuddered, putting some miles between me and this place, which sure looked abandoned. But if Dave Micker was back, it'd be up and running again soon enough. I sent a text:

How do you know?

My friend Crowe was the one to give me the news. And she would know. You see, we'd formed a tentative friendship in the process of leaving Dave's cult, all those years ago. We didn't know it was a cult. You never do know these things, going in. And we got out of it, not unscathed, but we got out.

When he'd died, it felt like a weight left our shoulders—a great evil had rid itself from the earth, forever. *Don't tell me he's back,* I thought. *I don't want to hear this.* I didn't want to have to try and re-kill a vampire, a member of the undead, and one whom I'd known for that long.

Let me take you back through the years with me; there I was, young, impressionable, hanging out with my friends, Kasey, and her younger sister, Morgen. We were all young libertines, and I was rebelling against my strict Catholic upbringing. And with my stepfather having recently died as I turned nineteen, I felt like I had to have some place to cling to. The Micker house became that place for me. It was like a non-stop party, people always coming and going, and having meetings, and coming up with ideas. Dave was the eternal, happy host.

I liked hanging out there and flirting with the boys and talking about role-playing and being in that creative atmosphere where Dave gathered fuel for his game characters. The latest one, a vampire named Tinker. He'd drawn out diagrams of Tinker's workshop. I couldn't believe that someone would put so much forethought into a game character. It amazed me. I thought he was a genius. And people flocked to him.

These people, he put to work. Some of them tended the garden, and others made breakfast, gave massages to his wife and to each other, vacuumed the place, and took care of all else that needed doing, at the house. I didn't realize that this was a buy-in to the cult. In fact, I didn't realize that it was a cult at all. But I was smart, and I read a lot, even back then. He'd told me it was a study group, and that he was ready to teach me the secrets of the universe, and I was enthralled, ready to be the willing acolyte in all this.

I passed Kilgore Road, the location of the old American River Grange Hall. That had been the first vampire hangout and gaming place. I didn't know all the details, but I knew that Dave had managed to get a few of his acolytes onto the managing board of the Grange, and so the game would be allowed there. They charged a fee in the form of a donation, and for this, you got bonus points, bonus 'weapons'; stats written on the backs of business cards, etc. These business cards, we'd put in Altoids tins and carried around with us.

The Grange was a fantastic place to LARP. It had a kitchen and a meeting hall on the bottom floor, and stairs that led to the top, where there was another meeting hall, this one with huge wooden thrones, one on either side. The outdoor area was also ours to prowl, and prowl we did.

At the time, I had a boyfriend, Jaycen, and his friend Mark, and the three of us were like the Three Musketeers of gaming. We played as a type of vampire called Gangrel, that was supposed to be more animal-like than the others.

But mostly, I hung out with the people who were there, and chatted, made friends, sometimes flirted—or others flirted with me—though Jaycen was very protective of me. With my life being in such shambles, I adored his protectiveness. I felt like I needed it. And I did, at the time. Nowadays, I was plenty strong enough, able to take care of myself. But back then, I'd been more timid, and there were others who exuded confidence.

There were those who were Dave's people. You could tell who they were—not knockouts physically, but when they came into a room, they were showstoppers. The women were drop-dead gorgeous, in heels and gowns, tattooed but they made it look like a million bucks. The men were powerful, often to the point of being intimidating, the kind of people you didn't mess around with, and they exuded it.

What could I do for now, but wait and see where activity flared up—at the Grange or the old golf course on Mine Shaft? I had no idea where Dave's old house was anymore. I'd thrown away that address and all memory of it, years ago. I called

Kasey a head-case and lost contact with her and her sister. Once I'd discovered the truth of the cult I'd been caught up in, I left it, for good.

And now, here I was, thirty-three years old, having to face the possibility of having to face an old friend/nemesis. I wasn't sure which he'd be, these days. What I'd heard was that he'd gotten in trouble in other states, in trouble with the law. But I didn't know all the details of that, either. I knew firsthand about his charisma, and what a magnetic personality he had. Along with the legendary vampiric power of 'glamour' over individuals, that could be dangerous. With the legends conflicting, how did you even kill a vampire, anyway?

Movies and books were always reinventing the rules when it came to how vampirism worked. I remembered even having read a book that explained that vampires weren't 'made,' but 'born.' *What in the world? That couldn't be true, right? But who knows?*

The radio personalities just wanted to chatter my ears off, talking about the interpersonal implications of this thing, even though romantic relationships were the furthest thing from my mind, right now. So, what did I know for sure?

Of course, legends couldn't always be trusted. I had proof of that. I'd always had this red birthmark on my upper lip. That was supposed to be a sure sign of vampirism. But thus far, I had yet to grow fangs and develop a thirst for blood. At any rate, at least the legends were a starting point. What they said about how to kill vampires was pretty common; a stake through the heart, garlic, silver, slicing off the head of the creature, using a cross, or forcing the vampire out into the sun.

By now, Jaycen was out of state, and Mark was off at college. If it came down to hunting down Dave Micker in vampire form, I'd be on my own. After all, who could I tell about something like this? They'd think I was insane, as many flat-out refused to believe what the news told them, dismissing it as tabloid news, like the story of Bat Boy. At any rate, I had weapons, but most of them were purely decorative, like the katana I'd bought at a martial arts tournament, years ago, or the Lord of the Rings sword that hung on my wall. I had a bow and arrows as well, but what good would those be, against a vampire? They'd be utterly useless unless I had that one-in-a-million shot and hit the vampire square in the heart with an arrow. *And even then, would that be the end of it?*

I stopped searching for physical things for a moment and searched my memory bank. I'd read a book on New Orleans vampires lately, and like so many other people, I'd just assumed that the legends of vampires were untrue. Just misunderstood happenings of peasants in the Middle Ages, who didn't know how the process of body decomposition worked. But there was one story of a vampire, that seemed like it had a kernel of truth to it. That one was the tale of Jacques Saint Germain; a man who'd been caught biting a victim in New Orleans, in 1903, and whose living space was searched, bottles found containing wine and blood. There were those who believed Jacques Saint Germain to still be alive. *Surely Dave Micker, with his love of books and the occult, would have heard of him?*

There were those who believed that he still existed, prowling the streets of New Orleans, asking for a light for his cigarette, saying, "It's a nice night out for Jack." *Had Dave Micker gone to New Orleans, found Jacque Saint Germain, and come back as a member of the undead?* It seemed like a far-fetched story, but it was possible.

I searched my closet for a set of clothes for my new vampire-hunting lifestyle. Someone had to do it, and that someone had to be me. So, I pulled out a pair of khakis, a pair of black socks, a watercolor-looking tank top, and a flannel overshirt. These days, I didn't dress too fancy. I figured that vampire hunting would be the opposite attire from what you'd wear to a vampire LARP, in the old days. I found an article that summed it up expertly, an article from The Globe and Mail, from 2005:

> There are teenage vampires stalking the
> high-school corridors and the city streets,
> but their fangs are store-bought, and few

have cultivated a taste for human blood. For almost all of those wannabe vampires with their chalk-white faces, black-lined eyes, blood-red lips and dark Victorian-era clothes, vampirism is more a fashion statement and a harmless way to thumb their noses at the establishment and their straight-laced parents than the murderous fascination with death, pain and the drinking of blood that arose in testimony during the Jonathan trial over the past several weeks.

What surprised me about this article, was that it was written in Canada, and yet, it had perfectly summed up the spirit of the time, all those years ago, here in California. As for that "Jonathan trial," all I found online was a summary about the killing that went on and suggested that mental disorders were to blame, combined with a disturbing fascination with vampire culture.

"My clothes are fine," I said to myself. I pulled the sword Sting, from the Lord of the Rings, off of the wall. It wasn't sharpened, but I didn't need it for slashing, I figured. The point was so very menacing that I'd still be able to use it to run someone through if I needed to. I had the scabbard, so I strapped it to my leather belt. Unfortunately, I hadn't updated my belts since the old days, so I had to go for the black studded leather belt I'd bought from Hot Topic. It was fitting, I supposed.

Would I be up against Dave or Tinker? I shuddered, remembering how the fictional Tinker character had created numerous traps to protect his workshop area, on that piece of graph paper—trip wires that would set off crossbows, and such. I shuddered. I have to protect my fragile mortality, and—more importantly, not get turned into a vampire, myself. *First,* I decided, *I'll check out the Grange Hall, and then, the old Mine Shaft golf course.*

But I couldn't just go barging in, as much as I wanted to. As for the Grange, I remembered what had transpired before, between Dave's crew and the older Grange members. How the Grange members were hip to what Dave's crew was doing, in getting rid of things like old Halloween decorations that Grange members had made, and such. Surely, they had no love for Dave Micker. I could use that angle to my advantage, surely. I shook my head. *No. Those elderly old Grange patrons won't help me fight vampires. Come on, now.* I knew better. *Those old folks will be at home, clutching their rosaries and Bibles, not out fighting the scourge.*

There was a better way. If Dave Micker had come back, he wouldn't hide. He'd start up the game again, and call his acolytes back to him, and gain new followers, and come back to gaming like a god, because this time, he would be. All I'd have to do was wait for a Friday or a Saturday night, and go to the Grange at night, dressed in black. I'd use some concealer on that red birthmark of mine and be a whole new person. And for now, I'd scout the area, and check out what was going on. That did sound better. But it would take so much more time. I took off the belt and put the sword back up on the wall. It was only Monday. I had a whole week, to wait. But this was the best way.

Finally, Friday night came. I dressed in a black shirt, black jeans, boots, makeup, and sunglasses, along with a couple of bracelets and a necklace of black stones. I wanted to blend in, not to look flashy. Back in the old days, I wanted to look flashy, to draw attention to myself. But not today. I drove by the Grange and saw that the activity was hopping—young adults crowded the outside. Others would be sure to be hanging out inside, and Dave Micker, well he'd be sitting inside, tucked away perhaps in the kitchen, or in the lower level, his followers having made makeshift walls of patterned scarves, creating a sort of tent-area for him to hang out in. Or perhaps he'd have taken one of the thrones upstairs.

I began to wish that I really had the powers that my vampire character had, back in the day—like invisibility. *What had her name been? Julie, perhaps?* I hadn't been quite so creative, all those years ago. Thankfully, I didn't recognize any of these folks.

The ones who'd been to a game with me, years ago, had moved on by now; had children, gotten married, gotten drawn into soul-sucking jobs that wouldn't let them do anything fun anymore, or moved away to other states. Their lives went on, and all this had been some kind of fleeting dream and nothing more. What charmed lives they led.

I parked the car and walked toward the Grange, stalking the darkness, as the darkness had stalked me. A young man asked if I had a light.

"I don't smoke," I replied.

"You're lame," he said, and he and his friends laughed.

Normally, it would have bothered me, but I let the words roll off like water. *He knows not what he does.*

I walked into the Grange, cash in hand, and though there was indeed someone at the table, taking cash as they had so many years ago, there was no Dave Micker. I looked around the room, trying to seem innocent, and look like I was searching for someone, wandering into the kitchen, again not seeing my target. So, I walked back to the stairs and took them all the way up. When I arrived at the top floor, it was as I'd remembered it, and to my right was the door that led into the main room with the thrones.

But all was dark and empty.

So, I'd have to go and check out the Mine Shaft golf course. I sighed. *I don't want to have to go out there and guess as to whether there's a game there, or when it will be.* I didn't want to have to ask around and find out.

I walked across to where a bench sat and remembered another time when I'd sat on this bench, talking with a friend at the time, my friend Ron.

We'd reconnected in recent days, over Facebook, but things were not as they'd been, before. Even he had to admit, that we didn't really even know each other. But back then, it had been like there was some magical connection. He'd given me a black scarf and a letter, and I held onto them with an admirer's ardor. But as I came to know more about Ron, and his life's transgressions, I burned that scarf. I wanted nothing to do with him.

I should have let my memories lie, and be the beautiful, fake little baubles that they were. *Reality sucked, badly.* No wonder there were so many people, through the ages, ready to delve into the fantasy that this LARP game represented.

A couple giggled to each other, and ran up the stairs, and then disappeared into the throne room across from me. They hadn't looked my way, and I truly felt invisible, blending into the furniture of this musty old place that belonged to my memories. *What am I even doing here?* I felt silly. *I'm no longer a part of this strange world.* My world now revolved around job searching and hoping for a better tomorrow than the fast-food realm I'd found myself serving, these days.

I rose and walked over to the stairway, resolved to check out the golf course, at the earliest opportunity. Even if I have to wait another week, that's fine. I'll be able to check it out at some point.

I grabbed hold of the wooden railing, and I saw Dave Micker at the bottom of the stairs.

He smiled at me, in recognition, despite my best attempt to conceal my appearance. His skin was white and clammy. His eyes were red. But in all other aspects, he looked as he had in that photo that was posted, at the date of his death.

And my blood ran cold.

Contributors

Glen Damian Campbell

Glen Damien Campbell lives and works in London. His writing has appeared in a variety of anthologies and magazines, these include Something Wicked Vol. One, 100 Doors to Madness, ODDisms, Bumps in the Road, Hybrid Moments: A Literary Tribute to the Misfits, and Zimbell House's anthology, *No Trace*.

Besides writing, his interests are music, history, film, and painting.

Michael Grantham

Michael Grantham is a writer of fiction who loves scary stories. Currently, he is traveling the world looking for inspiration for the next great horror icon.

Kathleen Halecki

Kathleen Halecki possesses a B.A. and M.A. in history and a doctoral degree in interdisciplinary studies with a focus on early modern Scotland.

Although born in New York, she currently resides in a seventeenth-century home in New England.

Her work can be found in The Copperfield Review, Shadows in Salem: Wicked Tales from the Witch City, One Night in Salem and the forthcoming, Shadows of Pendle.

Katie Krantz

Katie Krantz is a student and writer based in Atlanta, Georgia

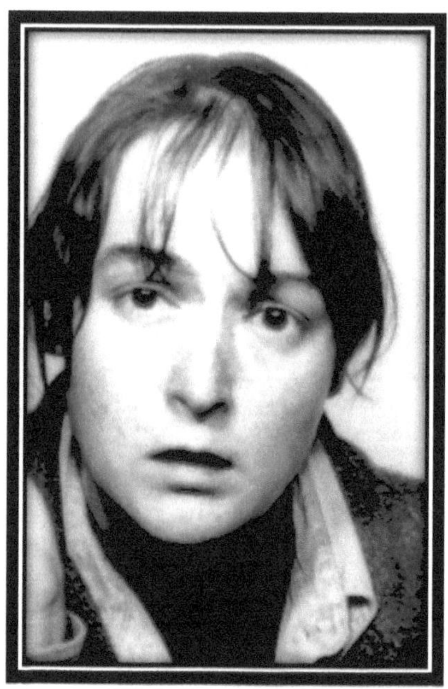

R. S. Pyne

Fuelled by strong black coffee and sheer bloody-mindedness, R. S. Pyne is a freelance writer/geoscience researcher/Mental Health First Aider from rural West Wales where the only traffic jams are sheep related!

Fiction credits include Mad Scientist Journal, Hungur, Phantaxis, Bête Noire and Vampires–Revamping a Classic Tale (2012 Norgus Press anthology).

Abiran Raveenthiran

Abiran Raveenthiran is a student at McMaster University and works as an Electrical Designer. He lives in Toronto, Canada with his family and a medium-sized dog.

He has another published work as a part of the Monkey Collective called, The Man in the Zoo. He is an aspiring author who was inspired to write by his favorite novels, *Game of Thrones* and *The Stormlight Archives*.

You can connect with Abiran on Instagram at @speedy_ravi.

Leslie D. Soule

Leslie D. Soule is a fantasy/sci-fi author from Sacramento, CA. She has an M.A. in English and is currently working on the final book of her fantasy series, *The Fallenwood Chronicles*.

Similar Anthologies from Zimbell House

The Mysteries of Suspense

Pagan

Tales from the Grave

Curse of the Tomb Seekers

Travelers

Dark Monsters

On a Dark and Snowy Night

The Key

Veil of Secrets

The Lost Door

Nocturnal Natures

The Neighbors

Why? A Collection of Mysterious Tales

River Tales

After Effect

Ghost Stories

No Trace

Coming Soon from Zimbell House

Not Anyone's Wife

Shifting

November Falls

Join our mailing list to receive updates on new releases, discounts, bonus content, and other great books from

Or visit us online to sign up:

http://www.ZimbellHousePublishing.com

A Note from the Publisher

How to Thank a Contributor

Dear Reader,

Everyone at Zimbell House Publishing would like to thank you for reading the *Midnight Rising*. If you would like to thank a particular contributor, the best way is to leave a review for them. You may do so by leaving one on our Goodreads page, under the *Midnight Rising* title, by using the link below:

http://www.goodreads.com/ZimbellHousePublishing

and be sure to mention the contributor directly.

Why should you leave a review? Reviews help budding authors build their credibility in the book industry. By posting a review on Goodreads, you help other readers find new authors they may wish to follow, and you never know, your review may end up on an author's website one day.

Friend us on Goodreads:
https://www.goodreads.com/ZimbellHousePublishing

Follow us on Twitter:
http://twitter.com/ZimbellHousePub

www.ingramcontent.com/pod-product-compliance
Lightning Source LLC
Chambersburg PA
CBHW021128070726
47591CB00014B/1699